TWELFTH GROUP OF ASSIGNMENTS

THE TERRORIST CAPER

IKE MORAH

Outskirts Press, Inc.
Denver, Colorado

TWELFTH GROUP OF ASSIGNMENTS -
THE TERRORIST CAPER

v1.0

Outskirts Press, Inc.
http://www.outskirtspress.com

ISBN: 978-1-4327-7105-8

PRINTED IN THE UNITED STATES OF AMERICA

Introduction

The stages of human life are like the steps or terraces leading to a mountaintop. Ike had reached this mountaintop – the prime of his life.

Though his early childhood trauma had helped to mould his character as an adult, he had unexpectedly come to be a decisive and relatively considerate character. He was not given to prevarication and though one would expect him to be very vengeful and bitter in his actions he was never so. He had remained considerate and kind despite being ruthless in matters dealing with the underworld.

He was barely a few days old when he lost his entire family to hoodlums and so nuns in a monastery where he was secretly taken brought him up. He was therefore, by all definitions, one of those people who had lost their childhood. He had neither kit nor kin and the only people he could ever associate with, as family members were the nuns in that convent. To him a man, who grows up and lives with women, nuns in this case, was like a fish out of water. He had therefore grown up as a loner and that was one of the reasons why he always kept to himself.

With quite a few assignments now behind him and age gradually creeping in, it was time for him to start going through some of those physical examinations that were medically recommended for men of his age. There were no families to check for familial traits that he could be on the watch out for. He was therefore bound to go through all possible examinations, and early too. When he was therefore asked by his doctor's office to book an appointment for a colon cancer screening, he did so very reluctantly.

He had always imagined that it was normal for a doctor to look inside someone's mouth to examine for any problems, but going to probe his rear end seemed to him like a violation of chastity. This might sound meaningless but then he was aware of the fact that pedophiles were prosecuted for the same thing, or maybe something not too far from that He had once come across a young boy who had been violated by a gay priest when he was eleven years old and that had helped to solidify his feelings against that probe. Just the thought of it alone always left an uncomfortable lump in his throat. In fact he had actually argued with the doctor over why they had not considered any other examinations or test instead of that to diagnose that possibility of one developing colon cancer. Having gone through the nuns he was also opposed to certain other examinations, especially a few that were done for the women. He knew a doctor who became a radiologist mainly because he loved to check out women's breasts during mammography. It was unfortunate that men had to go into that profession, but then there were now same sex enthusiasts who are rushing into that profession.

He did not actually think very much of gynecologists. He felt that they might even be worse. He was aware of men who were in that profession and he had wondered why the same men had not gone into midwifery instead. There must be something to it.

Anyway he had reasoned that the colon was not as important as the brain. He did not see why there was so much activity towards colon cancer when there were more deaths from the brain, which was hardly ever examined. The brain, according to him, was always connected with high blood pressure, Alzheimer's disease, heart attacks and strokes amongst many others and yet it was not receiving that much attention. Any of these could eventually result in death directly or indirectly. He felt that the brain controlled the rest of the body and so it should be given more attention than the colon. He had not yet been asked to go in for any brain examinations yet. Aneurisms and brain cancers had resulted in the death of a few people that he knew. He preferred brain scan to colonoscopy that was going to violate his rear end. He therefore found every conceivable reason to keep away from his gastroenterologist and he was successful at that.

To him, the medical profession had got its priorities

wrong since a healthy and well functioning brain was the foundation of mans existence. His will power, his plans, his mind as a whole and in fact every other action of the body, be it voluntary or involuntary, was under the control of the brain. He therefore used this as an excuse to travel out. He therefore escaped to the tropical resort island of Banyu. His doctor simply diagnosed his problem and claimed that he was suffering from anoractalophobia, and he let him go.

To most people who were familiar with Ike, and they were very few, he had turned into a peripatetic character. It is not that he was not used to traveling from one place to the other, but in recent times he never stayed long in any one particular place. It looked as if he was always in a hurry to visit everywhere. One of his friends had actually insisted that it was all because he had no obligations to hold him down in any one place. He was as single if not more single than a single dollar bill. He was therefore ubiquitously everywhere, if it could be put that way.

His get away to the island of Banyu was quite uneventful. It was a relaxing journey. He had traveled there in a vacation charter flight and he ended up in a small inn by the shore. He spent most of his early mornings watching the rising sun shoot her early golden arrows from down beyond the eastern horizon. Sooner or later it would rear its head and lighten everywhere and he had always found that to be an exhilarating experience. The cool morning breeze that always blew onshore from the ocean often further enhanced this feeling. Because he was always involved with destruction, one way or the other, this rising of the sun tended to give him that feeling of rebirth, which he cherished. Even so early in the morning he would remember how the same sun had set in the west the previous evening. He had never failed to notice that while setting the sun always had a bronze hue. He was therefore always caught up in and marveled at the rhythmical quality of these natural occurrences and at what hand it was that controlled them. To the atheists, it was natural coincidence, to religious believers it was God and yet to others they did not want to think of that at all.

This was his regular early morning ritual in this island. It was to relax on the sandy beaches to contemplate natural artistry and perfection. Most of the time it reminds him of the concept of god. As soon as the sun fully rises he would take off in a canoe with his fishing gear. He had once worked as an intern in a fishing trawler and that was how he developed interest in salt-water fishing. Fly-fishing had been his favorite sport on sea and he loved to watch the fries nibble at his bait all the time as he rowed close to the shore.

He had a very healthy appetite when it came to the roe or caviar and he preferred his seafood either broiled or fried. He was also particular about smoked salmon. A couple of his acquaintances would go for the bottom feeders like the flounder but he preferred those that fed towards the surface. He would cast his hook with a half sinker and then once in a while give some jerky and taunting pulls that always tended to attract the attention of the fish. Whatever he caught did not really matter because he was very likely going to throw it back into the sea.

Ike never wanted anything to do with crabs because he knew that they were the scavengers of the sea. To him, catching a crab was like catching a vulture. As for eating it that was something he compared with eating vultures and it should be forbidden. They were just as dirty and lowly as it could get.

Once he had tried to pull in a hundred- pounder, and the big fish pulled him with his canoe some half a mile into the sea as he tried without success to reel it in. He eventually let it go by cutting off the line and then rowed back to the beach. Once he returned from any of his fishing trips, he would lie down and bask on the sands for a while before going back to the inn to wash up and go for his lunch. The longest he ever went without alcohol was usually this half-day teatotalling.

He would usually have a light lunch and then head for the bar where he was going to remain till nighttime. He would hang around the bar till late in the night before going to bed. One young man that served in the bar ended up being his friend. He was one of those few servers who knew their ways around the drinks when it came to mixing them.

The drinking habit with which he was known started when he was in the military school. It was a common habit of the cadets. Their instructor, Colonel John Ben Eli, had once tried to dissuade them from always drinking but he was met with a stiff philosophical opposition. He once had to quote two passages from the Christian bible to explain to them that drinking was not a very good habit, but it was to no avail. He had quoted from the book of Proverbs:

> *"It is not for kings to drink wine; nor for princes strong drinks:*
> *"Lest they drink, and forget the law, and pervert the judgment of any of the afflicted.*
> *"Give strong drink unto him that is ready to perish, and wine unto those that be of heavy hearts.*
> *"Let him drink, and forget his poverty, and remember his misery no more."*
>
> (Proverbs chapter 31 verses 4 to 7)

In as much as they saw with this book in the bible, they all the same argued with the colonel about the exact interpretation of those verses. According to them the first two verses were not talking of the evil effects of alcohol, they were simply telling them those that should not indulge in drinking. They were not included there. Kings and Princes were not advised to drink and they were neither of those two. They then went on to explain that the next two verses were specifically on their side. It should be given to those who were ready to perish and who else would be ready to perish but they who were headed for the war fronts and were ready to die. Apart from that it was a well-known fact that whenever they hear of politicians and businessmen misusing public funds it hits them very hard. Why should they be off to the war fronts to sacrifice or lay down their lives in the interest of the nation while those two are at home milking the country instead? It is usually sorrowful to imagine and so the last verse actually knew what it was all about. They also went on to point out that alcohol served a dual purpose.

They pointed out that apart from it's helping them to drown and forget their sorrows; it also served another very important purpose. They did not fail to remind him that Saint Paul had prescribed it to his fellow servant and follower Timothy:

> *"Drink no longer water, but use a little wine for thy stomachs sake and thine often infirmities."*
>
> (First Timothy chapter 5 verse 23)

If it was of great medicinal value as recommended above, they had insisted, then it would be very stupid of them to leave it alone. Their worry should be to make sure that they did not take an overdose of it. Moreover it might amount to a disobedience of that particular command from the bible. Furthermore for it to be recommended above water lends support to why the first officially recorded miracle of the Lord was the turning of water into wine. He did away with water and changed it to wine.

The Colonel was however quick to point out to them that the use of the expression Kings and Princes in that quotation from the book of Proverbs was not in reference to physical, earthly or mundane nobilities. It was meant to refer to those who were noble in spirit, which in effect meant those who were going to inherit the kingdom of god. That was why the words kings and princes were used in reference to this kingdom. They were the good, the meek and the humble. It was just an allegorical usage of those words.

As for the medicinal use of wine, the operational and most important word there was "little". That was why a little bit of it could be found in many medications such as cough syrups and many intestinal preparations. In most of these cases, particularly as with extracts and many infusions, it was there just as a solubilising agent to help effect the uniform presence of certain ingredients in these concoctions. It was not usually there for the intrinsic medicinal property of the alcohol itself. He warned those of them who were already toying with the idea that alcohol had bactericidal properties and so was to be taken as an antibacterial agent or for those who intended to use it in place of prescription antibiotics to forget that idea. As soon as it is taken, the body will absorb it and it is both destroyed and passed out as such very fast. It will therefore not be there in any reasonable concentration to exhibit that property *in vivo.*

One of them, maybe jokingly, had also insisted that it also had another quality. According to him it had been found out that it was insecticidal or at least could act as an insect repellent. He claimed that this was proved when one of his friends got too drunk. It was claimed that he was so drunk that his blood alcohol level was way above the allowable limit. When they were sent to the bush to work, all the mosquitoes that feasted on his blood either dropped down dead or drunk.

He was eventually able to convince a few of them that the idea was to consume it in moderation. Ike was amongst those who went with this idea. In his own case however, he had to argue that moderation was a relative term. Different individuals dispose of alcohol at different rates, and in his own case, he was born with a system that tends to do away with it at a rather fast rate. He was for this reason hardly ever drunk. Being drunk was the endpoint with which moderation was determined. It therefore followed that he always took it in moderation. The Colonel did not see the use in pursuing this issue any further with him and so he let it be.

He would usually start off with a straight Cognac. It is the Remy Martin brand of course and he would send nearly half a glass of it down the hatch in one quick gulp. The boy would then go ahead and make him a mixture, which they had come to refer to as the usual. It was a devilish concoction of equal quantities of Jack Daniels Whisky, Johnny Walker Black Label Whisky, Aromatic Schnapps, Gordon's London Dry Gin, Jamaican Rum and any Martini. Each would be carefully and religiously poured down the side of the glass as if he was afraid that it might foam. It would be done with a steady hand and without any agitation. One could actually see the different drinks lazily swirling around each other in the glass. He would then hand this over to him with much care. He was usually so careful that he would actually be less careful in handling a premature baby. Ike would only take little sips from this with equal care and respect. He claimed that in this manner one would be able to taste each of the components of the mixture separately and yet together. Only a very discerning palate would appreciate this.

That would be Ike trying out his drinks in a bar. It had become a standard procedure for him.

This would remain his drink of choice till after dinner when he would incorporate into it a little bit of vodka and African illicit gin. The whole concoction this time around is swirled round in the glass and then flavored with a generous splash of Aromatic bitters. He often goes through three to five rounds of this before retiring for the night. His eyes will of course be blood shot, and he would be looking forwards to his hangover the following morning. This would of course be right before his nightcap. Whenever he asked for some tequila, the bar boy will know that it is getting to bedtime. This will be a short glass of very rare Mexican tequila, which he takes neat. That is usually taken on his way to bed.

This was his routine for about five weeks before he decided to go back home.

He had chosen to go back home at this particular juncture in time because he did not want to miss the swearing in of their new president. It was the swearing in that came after a gruesome campaign during which time he had been employed to help clean out the environment. There were assassination attempts on one of the candidates and it was with his help that this was avoided. It was the first time that this had happened and it was the candidate that he saved that won the election. He was not going to miss the swearing in for any reason whatsoever. He contacted the secret service and they reserved a seat for him. This was in the area reserved for very important personalities. Ike has never had any soft spot for politicians in general, but he was here for this one because of that part that he had played during the campaigns. He wanted to know how he was going to tackle the inaugural speech. He was known to be so eloquent that many looked up on him as the full embodiment of oratory. He however still had it at the back of his mind that no matter how good a politician might seem to be, he still did not merit an unconditional trust. He had claimed that they were just one of those necessary evils that the society had to live with.

When Ike arrived home, he checked into the ultra-modern *La Grande Femme.* This was a sparkling new five star hotel. It was so far the biggest and most modern hotel in the country. It had three thousand and two hundred rooms from a thirty two-story colossus. People see it as an architectural marvel and it was actually a marvel to behold. Its grandeur would simply take the breath away just by looking at it. It was all glass on a steel structure that looked very simple and yet too sophisticated to behold. Many had campaigned that it should be included in the Guinness book of world records for one thing or the other, or be listed as the eighth wonder of the modern world. It boasted of three pent houses and Ike had just checked into one of them. Each of these penthouses was like a home away from home and could boast of every single luxury amenity. In fact it was one of the few, if not the only, hotels in which the chef could come into the penthouse to whip up an award winning delicacy in its private kitchen. It had its own spa, living room area, bedroom area and gym amongst other amenities. He did not however utilize the opportunity that had to do with cooking. This was because he found out that all the chefs were female.

It should be remembered that he was supposed to be allergic to members of the opposite sex. It was not that he hated them, neither was it because he looked down on them, but it was because they always tended to throw him into a state of imagined insecurity. He had grown up in a monastery, which he preferred to call a nunastery. He lived amongst the nuns and he always itched to be liberated from them. Most importantly however is the fact that this attitude was a deliberate effort. To members of his profession, women always were there to cause distractions and these could often be fatal. He did not mind being around them but the closer they got the further he would tend to move from them, unless of course he wanted to make use of them. This however did not apply to one group and one group only – the nuns.

He got to the presidential lodge an hour early on the fateful inauguration day but the place was already full. He was there as one of the few who had helped to influence the direction that the elections had taken and so he was a very important personality. To him however it was just a casual event. When he presented his invitation card to the usher he was taken to his seat. He was more than pleasantly surprised at the position of the seat that was reserved for him. He was seated in the second row right in front of the presidential podium. The seat to his left was occupied by the secretary general of the United Nations Organization while to his right was the Secretary of state. The row in front of them was deliberately left vacant. He could not figure out why that row had to be vacant unless there was one of those superstitions to it. As he tried to sit down he bowed and greeted the secretary of state:

"Good morning sir." The man got up and they shook hands. They had met twice before and knew each other. One of the previous meetings was when the man helped to negotiate with him for one of his assignments.

"Good morning. What a pleasant surprise to see you Ike."

"It's the same with me. Long time no see."

"Where did you vanish to?"

"I was just travelling around and resting."

"You will surely need all the rest that you can get, at least in lieu of all the vigorous activities that you have been through."

"Thanks for that. You actually look fresher and well rested compared with the last time that I saw you. I guess that with the campaigns over you must have taken some time off to rest too."

"Thanks for that. In fact I took a one week vacation to recover."

"That was exactly what I tried to do myself."

The man was full of smiles and excited, but he finally turned around to introduce him to the United Nations Secretary.

"This is Ike mister secretary and without mincing words he is one of the people who have contributed most to the safety of our country. I am sure that you must have heard of him before."

The United Nations big whip then stood up too and shook his hands as if he was being introduced to one of those field marshals. He then greeted Ike:

"Good morning sir."

"And good morning to you too." Ike replied very embarrassed. He was embarrassed because he did not see why such a high ranking and older man should address him with the title sir.

"Which branch of the military were you originally in?" He asked as they sat down.

"I am not a military man as such but I used to be in the army. Presently I am retired."

The man was a politician himself. He knew all about Ike but he had to play it that way. The secretary of state then stepped in to comment more on him:

"Sir, he used to be like a one man army for us. I am sure that you can still remember that problem with the CRITOWO?"

"I can still remember that very clearly my dear friend. Don't tell me that this is the same one and very Ike!"

"It is him in flesh and blood."

"O my god." He shouted. "I did not in my wildest imaginations know that I will ever meet you in person."

With that he jumped up once more to shake his hands. The CRITOWO was a clandestine organization that had reared its head once with the aim of taking over the entire world especially its finances. It was Ike that took them down single-handed. Ike was a very modest and prudent character and he was beginning to feel uncomfortable. He had never liked to be praised for what he felt was his duty. The speech by the president was yet to come but he was already feeling uneasy and would like to escape the arena. Besides that, he was also beginning to get that his premonitory feeling. He was beginning to feel that something was going to happen, maybe another assignment! O no! he shouldn't have come there.

"Are you thinking of what I am thinking?" That was the sudden question that came out of him for the secretary of state.

"What are you thinking of?"

"I am not very sure of it."

The secretary of state then leaned over from behind him to the secretary general. They murmured a few words and nodded in agreement. Ike suspected immediately that something was in the pipeline for him. He always got wind of his assignments while in the bars but in an inaugural speech was a little bit unusual. He was very sure that it was going to end up with that. Many people had heard when he was introduced earlier on and so many eyes were now on him as well as a lot of murmurings and of course gossips. An announcement however made everywhere go hush. The president elect was about to come in for his speech.

When the president elect came in everywhere went silent for a few seconds before it burst into a loud deafening ovation on his appearance. It took the intervention of the national anthem to calm them down. He stood there and looked on with that usual smile on his face. Eventually he cleared his voice and started off. Apart from his commanding stature and presidential poise he was an orator! He had that gift of the command of both words, diction and language and it all came out with an outstandingly effective fluency. His ideas were all philosophical and they were perfectly interlaced with gracefully elegant poetic graphics. The entire crowd was held spellbound for a long time by the articulateness of this silver-tongued orator. His speech was comparatively short but he always went straight to the points as he laid down his rules, visions and aspirations for the country. Everyone agreed with his ideas. This had come after the incumbent chief justice of the nation's Supreme Court swore him in.

Just as he was rounding up his speech, the secretary of state turned round and invited Ike out for a round of drinks after the speech. Ike was not one who could refuse such an offer for a drink. The United Nations secretary General also volunteered to join them for the round of drinks. Ike had always insisted that it was not just unethical but also ungentlemanly for one to refuse an invitation to a drink. One thing had been crossing his mind all this time. He could not figure out why he had to be seated with the secretary of state instead of his sitting somewhere behind the president. It could be one of those changes that the new president promised that he was going to introduce. He still had his suspicions anyway. Maybe this was going to be the beginning of another assignment.

Their rendezvous was the cove. They had to make their way through the entire crowd of noisy patriots and everyone seemed to be agog with excessive happiness and great expectations. The cove was a lonely place. It was not one of those busy hotels or bars; rather it was a small building just next to the headquarters of the secret service. It was at the end of a blind alley and it was a very safe and exclusive place. Only very high-ranking government officials were usually allowed into it. He had been there in more than a few occasions before. They all entered the dimly lit lobby only to come face to face with the newly sworn in chief of the secret service. The place was so close to his new office that it would have been normal for him to be there. The only problem is that they should have each been off to one ball or the other for the night. He immediately knew that there was something in the air. His hunches were right. He had been set up.

Pleasantries were exchanged and everyone moved to one of the tables at the far corner of the lobby. It was the most remote table in the place. This place was the grapevine for members of the diplomatic corps, especially the foreign ones. Though it did not look like much from the outside, it was very comfortable inside. They were hardly off to the start of their very first round of drinks when the chief of the secret service cleared his voice and introduced the topic for the evening. He was the type of man who had no time to waste beating about the bush and he was also not given to too many words.

"Gentlemen, I hope that you all already know what I am about to talk about?"

"No," Ike replied right away. He knew that he was about to be introduced to another assignment, but that was the only way that he could show his displeasure at having been kept in the dark about it so far. It was bound to be so anyway, but all the same he had to protest.

"I am very sorry mister Ike. I should have given you an idea about this earlier on but I guess that you remember how it used to be?"

"I guess I do," he replied. He used to be with the secret service himself and so he was well aware of how secretive they could be. They used to be told that they had to be so secretive that ones right hand should never be privy to what his left hand was planning.

This was not a chance meeting. It had been prearranged and that was why he had to be at that very position during the inaugural.

"I am very sorry for any inconvenience that this might have caused you. I apologize again, please forgive me for that." That was the chief speaking on behalf of the rest.

"Don't mention it. I am alright with the arrangement."

"I am almost very sure that you might have been wondering as to why you were seated between these two gentlemen."

"I have for that matter. It is just that I couldn't confirm the situation right away as to what was happening."

He felt very bad and disappointed in himself though he did have a slight suspicion. He should have been able to figure it out right away and even what they were up to. With the secretary of state and the United Nation's Secretary besides him he should have guessed – a multinational problem.

"One can't always win them all."

"I agree with you."

"I am not the person who was mandated to tell you what we called you out for, but the president elect had asked us to contact you. He wanted to ask whether you could help us out with one particular problem but it is the secretary of state who will give you the gist of the matter.

"I can see that it must be something very important."

"Yes, and that is why even the head of the United Nations is here with us."

"Let's hope that it is something that I can handle."

"I am very sure that you will be up to it, moreover we intend to leave all our amenities at your disposal."

It was at this stage that the secretary of state came in to give a detailed summary of the problem.

"It's all about terrorism." He said.

"I hope we have no threats?"

"No, but it is getting out of hand, and it might soon get to us too. We have tracked all their recent activities and it all points to the fact that they might soon turn their attention to us. We therefore felt that our best line of defense right now will be a preemptive strike. We know how they are funded and we know who is organizing them and so we figured that it might be wise for us to attack from both sides. We were hoping that it might be successful and might then put the threat to a stop at least for the mean time."

It was at this stage that the chief of the secret service reached under the table and pulled out a small brief case and then said:

"Here we have the story so far."

It was handed over to Ike and he was asked to scan through the contents right away. They were for his eyes only, which meant that he had to go through every thing there and then and hand back the case to the man. It wasn't just a few jottings as he had expected but an entire dossier. It was almost the length of a small book but the instruction was for him to just scan through them. He was used to that. He therefore went ahead to read what he saw there.

Terrorism

When he opened the brief case what follows is exactly what he read from the papers within it, and of course they were for his eyes only.

"Several years ago during an international conflict we took a step that we now consider to have been a major mistake and blunder. At that time it was one of the brightest moves that the army could have made. We trained a few tough individuals to be an elite strike force from the commando unit. They were each individual fighters and their work was to knock out enemy positions from within enemy territories or from behind their positions. They were trained as irrational animals whose only aim was to seek out the enemy and destroy them. At the end of the war they came back victorious for they had contributed in no small measure to the success of the war. However the war was over and their services were no longer needed. They could not fit in with normal people and with time they had become very dangerous and the government had no way of dealing with them. They were all eventually loaded into a war ship with a time bomb in its hull and sent out on a mission to seek out treasures for the fatherland. Their idea was that the ship would blow up and sink in the middle of the ocean and that would be the end of them. Fate however had a different plan for them.

By the time that the explosives detonated, about two days later, they were raiding a cargo ship in the middle of the ocean in search of gold and that was how they were saved. They soon figured out what had been planned for them and so they decided to remain in the sea as pirates. They raided ships indiscriminately but they were particular with those belonging to the country. Eventually the few that survived ended up at Aridopolis, which was the country that lost the war. There they recanted their story and ended up setting up base. They had amassed a lot of wealth. Their ultimate aim was to exact vengeance on their own country which did not only refuse to appreciate their sacrifices to them but also tried to eliminate them. They eventually set up their own organization known as the ADELA. No one seems to know exactly how they came by that name.

Now that the government had learnt their mistakes they decided to set up a modified form of that training program and that was the strike force of which you used to be one.

The ADELA went into business ventures all over the world and as of now they are richer than some countries. Their most lucrative venture in the sea was when they took out the ship carrying the crown jewels of many royalties around the world. They were on their way for a world crown jewel exhibition. It was rumored to be worth about fifteen billion dollars and it was just this handful of men, who were used to and sworn to a frugal existence that controlled it. Their main headquarters was the caves and catacombs in the mountainous regions of this country. Their leader was the unassuming but charismatic Liska Dangwurunbalka – a name which he could have coined for himself. This man eventually tried a bit of anagrammatic rearrangements of the letters of his name to arrive at the more pronounceable name by which he is now known – NIDAL.

Though Nidal was just an individual, his place of abode was often considered as a country of its own. He had such organizational and convincing skills that he managed to get a lot of the condescending political organizations all over the world to look up to him. His main duty therefore seemed to be an attempt at destabilizing governments. He trained these groups in terrorist activities and even funded a lot of them. You must be familiar with his set up because it was his main training school that trained you when they were captured in the front. This write up is just for you."

Ike knew exactly what he was talking about. Most of his training came from this group. They had once captured him in the front when he was in the marines. They recognized his potentials and so rather than kill him they tried to brainwash him and utilize his abilities to their own advantage. Unfortunately for them, he turned against them at the end.

"Nidal is a problem and he had been involved in various clandestine activities and below are a few of them and the methods that he had employed for those ones.

His initial involvement was in the field of political assassinations. He was the contractor that provided assassins for such jobs. With time however he changed his mind. He took it upon himself to assassinate the leaders of any countries where their policies were not in line with his ways of thought. He was a religious fanatic. In the republic of Samara he had organized the opposition into a formidable force before he went in for the kill. He got their Prime Minister assassinated. He was killed during a speech, with a high-powered rifle that was used from the window of an abandoned apartment some one hundred and fifty yards away. In order to cover up his tracks, another assassin who was in the police force killed the shooter. Investigations went on for over two years and when it seemed to be getting too close to home he got one of his suicide bombers to own up to the whole thing. The man was caught and detained. The policeman went free. However on the first night that the confessor spent in jail he died. His body was found hanging from the roof of his cell in the morning. He had used his bed sheets to produce a hangman's noose. It was already too late when an autopsy report revealed that he had been mysteriously strangled before the hanging. The case was getting too hot to handle and so it was closed. The killer had hanged himself and that was the final verdict.

About three assassinations later, a political vacuum had been created in the country. The time was now ripe and the opposition leader simply stepped into the empty and abandoned shoes of the former leader. The country thereafter became one of his most devoted allies.

In the case of Ridastan, they had lost three presidents in quick succession and chaos had ensued. He had previously armed the opposition group and somehow or the other he had gotten them to view it as a religious war despite the fact that they were of the same faith. They simply wanted a more theocrtically-oriented ruler. A civil war therefore started off between the northern and the southern parts of the country. It took an entire sixteen years for this to come to an end. What had he gained from all this? He supplied arms to either side. It was later discovered that he had his fingers one way or the other in more than a dozen civil disturbances that were going on all over the world.

Having set up a few of these favorable regimes, it was time for him to manipulate and exploit them. Any time he foments trouble we will be blamed for it by this group and for that reason we are looked on as problem causers all over the world.

Wanton destruction of property and killings had become commonplace in these countries. In each case it was either to discredit a regime that they did not like or just to punish them. They have been linked to the bombing of railway stations, which are oftener than not carried out at peak traffic hours. In such instances many lives are lost as well as property. The same have been done with popular hotels where the same pattern is followed except for one small difference. In this case they will end up taking hostages for which they might demand for ransom or just want to exchange them for any of their people that had been caught.

They have been known to blow down imposing and strategic structures, buildings and dams just to make their presence felt. They have been known to blow up commercial aircrafts for the same purpose, and once they had actually hijacked one. At another time when they were flushed out from one of their hideouts they retaliated by firing missiles at ships in the high seas and that way they actually managed to cripple even two war ships. They however made a lot of money hijacking commercial cargo ships and oil tankers and then asking for money to release them. They had once bombed a sports arena during a game. This was not for money but just to show that they were only protesting on how one of their enemies was allowed to participate in the events. In one particular case they had stormed into the arena with guns blazing. Ten officials and thirty athletes lost their lives in that attack, as for the spectators; the number was put at too many.

To make sure that they could make trouble between different religious groups they would once in a while burn down houses of worship. The affected group will always blame the incidence on any other group that they did not like. In short their main aim was to go about and sow those seeds of discord between groups. This was not just done with the different religious groups in mind but also the different ethno- linguistic groups in the area. He was known to attack local markets in particular linguistic or ethnic areas with the hope that these groups would blame their misfortunes on their opponents. He had become particularly successful at these.

About half of their registered members were suicide bombers and they killed without any conscience at all. These people were recruited from different groups. As for the female recruits they concentrated on those who had lost their husbands and families in these ongoing conflicts, especially the wars. In short any war at all was actually there to create favorable conditions for the recruitment of suicide bombers. They were usually recruited with the hope that they will be given the opportunities to avenge the loss of their loved ones. This would be presented as doing a good service to the people. He also bought young boys even while still babies with the claim that he was sending them in for adoption. These were let to grow up and indoctrinated as well as brainwashed. This was the most dreaded of the groups. They had no regard for life, not even their own. Their only aim in life is to die for the course of others while rooting out 'evil'. At other times his recruiters would go from one sweatshop to the other to pick out those workers who were already disgruntled. These ones usually went straight to their training camps.

Many rogue regimes have come to support them, mainly because they had the money to dole out. They have in this way made their way into the acquisition of a few nuclear weapons from such regimes. In other instances, regimes that wanted these weapons would go through them to acquire them. Others still hire assassins and suicide bombers from this organization. It was claimed that in the field of international politics there were no provisions for permanent friends or permanent enemies. It was ones needs that were paramount in any relationships. Many countries therefore still dealt with them one way or the other.

There were indirect contributors to his cause. Many countries provide safe havens for him and his followers, either for monetary and other rewards or just as a means of making him look the other way. They have also infiltrated the governmental set ups of some countries. In some it is their investments that are the attraction, but in one particular case, two of their judges were secret members of his organization. It is from such countries that they launch most of their attacks. A couple of other countries simply bankroll them with the hope that they have bought them off. These were never attacked for any reason whatsoever.

From the above it is obvious that the organization is evil and if left alone it might lead to the destruction and downfall of most of our viable democracies. If this cankerworm that is eating up the basic fabric of our societal existence is not rooted out now, then it might as well be a signal for the demise of human ruler -ship as we know it."

This was an account of what had been written in the file that was in that brief case. As soon as he finished the last page the chief of security asked him:

"Any questions so far?"

"No."

"Do you need any clarification on any of the issues presented there?"

"None for now."

As you can see, we are very much on the edge and many countries are going to be affected and they have been looking up on us to help them out. It was therefore suggested by the president elect that we should contact you and find out whether you cold be able to help us out once more."

Ike looked out through the open window as if in very deep thought for a few minutes. The clouds that had shifted their positions now allowed a few snowflakes to float down as the sun shied further away towards the horizon. Then suddenly he stiffened and said:

"Ok!"

"Ok what?" Asked the secretary of state.

"I'll take up the assignment."

The tension in the room, which had been very close

to being tangible, eased off all at once. Everyone began to smile, and for the first time since he began to scan through the papers they each remembered to take a sip of their drinks. Finally it was the chief of intelligence who talked:

"When do you think that you could resume?"

"When I am ready I will inform you."

"Please when you are ready we will like you to give us an idea of what it could cost as well as what help that we could render." The secretary to the United Nations then came in with his own contribution:

"The cost should not be any problem. As you can see it is something that is going to affect the whole world. I therefore intend to raise money from as many countries as possible. Whenever you are ready just tell me the amount and I will get it ready. I don't intend to negotiate with you and I don't intend to leave it for your country alone. "

"Sir, you don't have to worry yourself about that. Whenever the assignment is over feel free to give me whatever you believe will be adequate. To me, money should not be an issue. I have tried to imagine that what I have now might last me a couple of lifetimes over. Should I need any help I will try to contact you, and thanks."

The secretary general was not totally surprised because that agreed with what they had told him about Ike in the first instance. There was no fanfare about the whole thing as they all got up and went their various ways. For Ike that was the beginning of another assignment.

The Initial Investigation

A monster had been created and unleashed onto mankind and it knows neither friends nor foe. This is Nidal and his organization was the ADELA.

They operated from various unimaginable and unlikely places, which included many underground cities. These included the defunct catacombs in various countries, elaborate sewer systems, abandoned alleys and mines, caves and many more. No one could tell for sure where he operated from at any given time. His whereabouts were therefore a matter of guesswork. He was as elusive as a ghost, and being very much more single than a dollar bill without any family ties he was as free as if not freer than air. He was an itinerant and ubiquitous terrorist and a master schemer. He was therefore always one step ahead of any of his opponents. Ike's first line of action was therefore to try and locate this elusive creature.

It should be remembered that Ike was once trained by a group of terrorists in the deserts. Though this group had been after him because of the havoc he had reeked on them as he left, they were going to be his first port of call in the quest for information. Also it could be recalled that they had sent him out to wipe out an enemy group of soldiers during a fight. It turned out that the people he was to help them wipe out were his own people and so he turned the tides on them. He wiped out the entire battalion that he went with and then ran back home to his people. They were of the opinion that they had succeeded in brainwashing him but they were wrong.

It had been many years since he trained there and his physique had changed a lot, but to make assurance double sure, he was going to be there *in cognito.* He employed the help of some film industry makeup artist. He ended up with his face looking slightly different and he was now going to travel as a different person. It took an entire week for this new man to arrive and he loved what he saw in the mirror at the end. There was no way that he could recognize himself not to talk of others recognizing him. Nonetheless he decided to test it out before leaving.

When Ike came back from Hollywood he checked back into the Hotel la Femme, but this time around it was as Alhaji Abu Maliki, prince and regent to the throne of the Arabic kingdom of Daura, which used to be a Caliphate of Petroluta. He had arrived in a white kaftan complete with his tribal kaffiyeh. He also had two golden teeth and he always smiled to show them off. No one in the hotel recognized him, not even the bar man. To be sure that no one suspected him at all, he came in with his own bottles of spirits and drank alone in his room. Outside the room he restricted himself to water and non-alcoholic drinks alone. He also changed his voice and spoke with a little lisp.

The secret service had not heard from him for some time and so they decided to plant a lookout in the hotel for him. They were certain that he was still around but they failed to see him. Stephanie was the girl that they sent over to watch out for him. Stephanie was full bodied with an uncannily attractive face. It was the type of face that would always make one turn round for a second look. Most of the people, especially the men, in the hotel took her as the new girl around. Maliki on his part did not see her that way. From the first time he was convinced that she had something to do with the service. There was that invisible persona, which they all had, and Maliki would never miss it, after all he was one of them.

It was obvious that Stephanie did not recognize him but he wanted to make sure that his cover was fool proof. One afternoon he went over to her table to talk to her:

"Asalamalekum." He greeted in a flawless Arabic accent when he got to her table.

"Amalekusalam." She replied in a fairly good accent, which was infused with an inquisitive smile.

"Can I join you on your table?"

"O, you speak English? Sure sit down please."

"Yes I speak a little bit of English. I have a B.A. Oxon."

"You have a bachelor's degree from the University of Oxford? You must be very intelligent. Not too many people can graduate from there."

"Nowadays money can achieve anything you know."

"I like your straightforwardness."

"What else can one do with the help of Allah?" This was spoken with an Oxfordian drawl with a little bit of Arabic lilt.

"I understand. I fully understand. My name is Stephanie."

"What a lovely name! I am Prince Abu Maliki."

"Are you from which country again?"

"Daura."

"Aha. That oil rich country. You must be very loaded."

"I am not complaining."

"That must be why your skin looks so smooth and supple. Incidentally you happen to be exceptionally handsome."

Maliki had now realized that she was getting rather nostalgic. But that was the effect that he always had on women.

"Thanks for that. How I wish that you could see my junior brother, maybe that will make you change your mind as to how handsome I am."

"About how handsome you are?"

"With him around you might find me comparatively ugly."

"But rich all the same?"

"Well I guess that you might be right there."

"What do you do for a living Stephanie?"

"I am a teacher."

"It shows."

"How?"

"Only a teacher could be as well mannered and as beautiful as you are both at once."

"Do you really think that I am beautiful?"

She asked this question as if she did not mean it, but she was touching off her hair as she asked it. She also brought out her makeup kit for a little touch up.

"If I were at home I would have brought you in to be the first amongst the members of my harem."

"You're right" She retorted with a deliberately sexy chuckle. Maliki knew that he was getting on to her, but then she suddenly asked:

"I hope you won't be offended, but how many wives do you have?"

"In my place our custom does not allow one to mention how many wives or children he has. When one does so it would make it look as if they were just part of his possessions, which they are not."

"That's very interesting. I have never thought of it that way."

"Yes we are all equals. It is just that I happen to be the most equal amongst the equals."

"I completely agree with you and I praise you people for that."

"Can I buy a drink for you?"

"No thanks. I am alright with this."

"Too bad. You see in my place we do not drink alcohol, but when I saw you I thought of having one with you."

"I hope I have not disappointed you?"

"Not at all. It's just that I had imagined myself having a drink with you."

"Actually it is not that I am a teetotaler. I just don't happen to be in the mood for a drink. Anyway I am sure that it will not do any harm to keep you company. I could as well have one drink of whatever you had in mind to drink."

"Thanks a million. You just made my day."

With that Maliki ordered two glasses of straight Remy Martin cognac. When the drinks arrived he decided to make sure that he was going to be seen as a gentleman. It is not that he was not exactly a gentleman, but whenever it came to the issue of drinks, he was not always the most prudent drinker, though he was never drunk. This time around however caution or prudence, together with circumspection and judiciousness were going to add a more favorable image to the particular persona that he wanted to present. It was going to be a deliberate attempt at personal presentation.

He eventually came up with one of those his disarming smiles as he lifted his glass up to his eye level:

"Cheers." He intoned quietly.

“Cheers.” She replied.

“To us.”

It seemed that this second addition to the toast was able to put her on the alert. Her reaction gave her away as a very good agent.

“Excuse me.” That was what came out of her right away. She then got up and was gone in a jiffy. She returned some three minutes later only to apologize for her impromptu exit. According to her, she was hard pressed and so she had to rush off to the ladies room. Maliki knew that she just wanted a little time away from him in order to plan her next move. She did not want to be caught unawares by this handsome prince. It was even possible that she just had a message.

“What are you here for?” She suddenly asked.

“I am just on my way home from a summit, but I figured that I could as well take a few days off and rest here before continuing on my journey home.”

“I wish you lots of luck on your stay. I hope the summit went well?”

“It went better than I had expected.”

“On oil?”

“Yes.”

“OPEC I guess?”

“You are very right and thanks. How I wish that you could hang around and help show me around the town.”

“I would have loved to help you out, but due to family obligations I might not be chanced.”

She said this while making sure that Maliki got a very good view of her expensive wedding ring. That was what she went out for. It was an ambitious eighteen-carat gold ring, probably made of white Russian gold, from its looks. There was a lone fiery red ruby set at the center; otherwise it was a very simple looking ring. It however had the inner edge towards her encrusted with many tiny emeralds, which made it a very expensive one. She did not look like the type that could afford that unless they were all fake stones. Maliki understood what it was all about. She wanted to be left alone. She did not want to get any closer to him; otherwise she might succumb to that temptation. It was a very wise and loyal move. He intended to respect her intentions.

"Actually I was only joking. I should be leaving the country first thing tomorrow morning."

"Congratulations on a fruitful journey. May we have one more set of drinks to that?"

She said this now getting a little bit more relaxed and at ease.

"We will just do that and I will get home in peace, Allah being willing."

"I will say Amen to that because I know that he will be willing."

"Thanks again. I guess I have to rush through this glass and run to my room to pack for the morning before I start feeling tipsy. I am very happy and much honored to have met you. I hope you don't mind if I give you my phone number. You can always contact me in the future if you need anything. Anything at all. With that they exchanged cell phone numbers and parted ways. Of course Ike had given her the first number that came from his lips – it was a fake number.

Ike was very satisfied. He had just confirmed that his disguise was perfect and so he was ready to take off for another assignment.

From Dambatta to Aridopolis

The following morning Ike took off as he had planned. He took a flight from the airport and went through Zubistan to his final destination Dambatta. It was nearly a twenty-four hour flight. It was also as uneventful as it was long. He had left the country without the knowledge of the people who sent him. He felt that if he informed them about his where about someone or the other might leak out the information. It was therefore for security reasons that he did not tell them that he was off on the assignment. He had however informed them that whenever he was ready or needed their help he would call from the international mobal telephone number that he used with his cell phone.

Dambatta was a fairly big country with only one big town, which was their capital. I t had the same name as the country. The rest of this country, which was landlocked, was either desert or semi desert. It was therefore a fairly unforgiving country when it came to its climate. It was in this very desert area that the terrorists trained Ike when he was captured in the war front. He had been here before when he came to obtain information from an old friend. It was not going to be easy to go back to the same man and that was why he had to employ this new strategy – the strategy of disguise. He had tried it before.

He left home and arrived at Dambatta as Abu Maliki, the sole survivor of an unfortunate village after a missile attack by a more powerful nation. He was from Kongo-lam. He had come to Dambatta to seek refuge. The best way to come in contact with the information that he wanted was to locate and join a suicide bombing school. This was of course part of the school where he was trained before, though it was a very long time ago. In this country he changed from the hard drinking Ike to a tea totaling religious fanatic. He was there to seek ways of avenging the death of his people. He was a much-weakened man who had no more hopes for the future to whom life was worth nothing. He was the type that was often referred to as, "the living that will find death a better alternative." He was alive but death might actually be more enjoyable than his life.

He made sure that he circulated around those areas where he would be noticed very easily, especially where people gather in the evenings. Mosques and other religious arrears were his targets as well as sports arenas and open markets. At other times he would pose as a beggar. Most importantly however, he knew exactly how to recognize the recruiters and he made sure that they always noticed him. For three full weeks things went on that way till he decided to change plans.

Many registered to join one or the other of the many religious schools that abound here and so manage to enter the training school from there. The training school would come there to recruit from amongst them. He therefore enrolled in one of the schools and within a few weeks he had become the most vociferous student in the school. He spoke a lot against the practices of their government, but he was particular with those foreign governments that had policies that were not very favorable to them. It was not too long before he got them to organize for more frequent visits to the school. During one of those visits he was opportuned to meet with the recruiter and he did not want to miss that opportunity. He therefore went closer to the man and saluted him:

"Morning sir!"

"Good morning mister man. How are you feeling today?"

"Very well, thank you and I hope to be alright by the grace of Allah."

"Thanks be to him and what can I do for you?"

"I heard that people could ask for conversion to your unit from this school if one so wished."

"Yes and no."

"How could that be? You are confusing me."

"Yes we do. But no because it does not necessarily be into the army."

"But it will have to be associated with the army one way or the other?"

"Yes."

"Then can I opt for it if I could be allowed to join."

"What is your educational background?"

"I have a master's degree in human psychology though my first degree was in religious studies."

"What have you been doing since you left school?"

"Teaching."

"So why have you decided to abandon that profession and come here?"

"A missile struck my small village of Kongolam and erased it from the face of the earth. Everyone was dead and I was the only survivor and that was when I decided on vengeance."

"That seems to be a fully justified resolve."

"I don't mind what I join as long as I have the opportunity to reek vengeance. I had joined the religious school because of their Arabic study program. That was one of the subjects, which I was not proficient in and so I was there also as a part time teacher. I give tutorials at night to the juniors."

"We will not disappoint you. With your qualification we can easily get you into the officer's corps."

"I don't really mind at what level I am admitted as long as it will get me closer to them."

"You see, if you come in as a member of the officer's corps you will be able to rotate from base to base.

Eventually you might be able to recruit and train your own militants yourself to help you out. I just have that feeling that you will make a very good officer material."

"I will remain indebted to you if that happens."

"As an aside, what was the name of that your town again? I feel that I can detect a little bit of the Matamaye accent."

"You are right about that. My father is from Matamaye but we are from a matrilineal clan and so I come from Kongolan that is my mother's village. We were there to visit my mothers family when the attack took place." He was of course lying. That question had come, and was meant to take him unawares but he was equal to the task. He knew that the recruiter wanted to be sure of him, and he was ready for that. He then continued:

"But how did you manage to recognize that our accent?"

"I've had two other recruits in the past that came from there and they were both good."

"In short I will be taken?"

"Just as I had hinted before, yes. We do not arrange for any formal interview or examination. We do not even organize any rigorous background check as could be warranted by our mission. The reason why we do not worry about that is that if anyone disappoints us, all we have to do is to take him out."

"That seems to be fair enough. If taken when can I start?"

"Why don't you come back to this office around five in the evening and I will be able to give you a definite answer by then."

Ike knew that his trap had sprung. He had lived as a homeless beggar from a neighboring country before entering the school and he was sure that these men had been on the lookout for him. According to his stories, the loss of the entire Maliki family had turned this once cowardly, fainthearted, lily livered and terminally timid Abu into a fearless, vengeful human. All that he now desired was to be trained in such a way that he would be able to get to, and carry out his act of vengeance. He had told the recruiting officer that at the religious school they initially called him "sissy the cold wimp", and that he was never very happy with that name. He had seen others that he had regarded as spineless invertebrates, but it was this that annoyed him so much that he changed overnight without even being aware of the fact that he had changed.

Bravery had therefore come to be his middle name and he was ready to sacrifice his life to achieve his aim. He had turned very courageous, bold fearless and even daring. He had become so bold that he had single handedly beaten up and chased away a gang of thieves that were raiding one of the homes that was very close to their school. Most of his schoolmates now looked at him as a born again man with all the guts and balls that seemed to make audacity a common word. Though he was usually crafty, guarded, hesitant and nonprecipitacious in his deliberations and actions, he had been turned by these prevailing circumstances into something else. He had become that man of action, the man with only a few words. To him, action now speaks louder than words and he had no time for those words.

When he came back to the recruitment office in the evening he was told that he was free to come in and start training with the new batch of recruits the following day. He accepted the offer right away. The alternative was to wait for another three months when the next batch might come in, but that wait was going to be too long for him.

There were no events of particular interest during the three weeks training except that he excelled in all areas. They did not realize that he was the same Ike who used to be the best in the school. In fact his problem was on how to hold back so that he does not look better that their instructors themselves. He struck up very close relationships with virtually everyone there, especially the officers, since he was soon going to be one of them. He also made mental notes of even the minutest details of anything that he came across. By the time the three weeks training was over he had become pretty sure of how to track down Nidal – the kingpin and mastermind of the entire organization.

Most of the recruits here, especially the non-officer materials, trained as suicide bombers. This was because the foreign enemies were more in number and better equipped than they. They therefore had no other alternative than to hit them through suicide bombing. It was the simple logic of one life for more than a few. This was how all those clandestine activities came to being. They were trained on how to rig out crude roadside bombs. These were usually detonated with attached clocks as timers and at times cell phones were used to detonate them. The suicide bombers themselves would rig out their own and they were trained on how to wear them undetected and on how to blow themselves up with them. They also had a flight simulator in the training camp and with this they could turn out crude pilots that could help them to either blow up planes midair or highjack them. Above all, there was an attempt at indoctrinating them through various methods of brainwashing. This made them very loyal as well as deadly.

Maliki graduated after specializing in ambush tactics. Towards the end he had made sure that he stayed somewhere towards the middle of the class and this was on purpose. He wanted to take attention out of his way moreover he wanted them to get the impression that he was itching to go out and avenge his loss. He had hoped that they would think that this eagerness was beginning to affect him since he was beginning to get very anxious. He got them there. They would very often come over to advice him that he still had all the time in this world for his goals and so he should take it easy. It was a normal reaction amongst many of the students who came in like he did. They were thirty in the class and twenty-five trained as suicide bombers. Amongst these potential suicide bombers were twelve women and three ten-year-old boys. Their aim was martyrdom. For some it was also just a way of providing for their families. There was an insurance premium of fifty thousand dollars for the family of anyone that lost his life that way. The average annual salary in this country was only ten thousand dollars. It was therefore like one offering his life to make his family one of the rich ones around. Most of the women were those that had lost their spouses to the enemy.

As a graduating, intelligent, motivated and enthusiastic officer, he was privileged with certain secrets that were not available to others. They were to be re-commissioned after their first successful assignments and this was going to be by none other than Nidal himself. It was at this stage that they were informed that there were about six different camps from where they operated and that they could be posted to any of these camps to operate from there. For him to be present in their final re-commissioning meant that he would be hiding out somewhere or the other within Dambatta during that period. Dambatta was of course his main base though he was rarely ever there. It was officially his world headquarters.

Abu Maliki's first assignment was to take out a United Nations outpost between the borders of Dambatta and

Uzakistan. It was a small observatory outpost made up of just a small group that was about three platoons strong. Their duty was just to observe the boundary between the two nations and make sure that none attacked the other. Should there be any attack they were to be able to tell who broke the truce between them.

Ike was given the option to take three other militants along with him for the operation. Initially he had opted to go it alone but he was prevailed upon to go along with them. It was late in the evening when they got ready and left for the outpost. These soldiers were peacekeepers and so there was no reason to take them out. The school however felt otherwise. They were hired to take them out so that war could resume without anyone knowing who had started it. His eventual decision was therefore to scare them off rather than kill them. They got there very late at night and he got his three militants to take cover under a bush while he sneaked into the camp. He made his way to the camp commandant's tent. It was right in the middle of the camp of six tents and it was the smallest.

The commandant was alone in his tent and just like a ghost he entered the tent and sneaked in to behind him. He was reading a book on ambush techniques when he suddenly covered the man's mouth from behind him and wrestled him to the ground. He then produced his pistol and pointed it to the man's forehead. It was Agnes, that his faithful companion, and he had kept her existence a secret in the school. Agnes had been his favorite and only permanent companion through his various adventures and she was once more ready to act. She was however only being used to ensure silence and she knew that from her master.

The commandant was a British officer and so he started off to speak to him rather slowly in that his Oxfordian accent:

"Please don't be afraid, I am not an enemy. I have only come to seek your help."

With that he took the chance to let him loose. The officer still looked too surprised and scared. A man who was surely of an Arab descent had just taken him hostage when they were supposed to be enemies for the mean time. He just could not figure out why he should call himself a friend. To make it more puzzling too the man spoke in his own very accent and that made him feel that he was only dreaming.

"Who are you?" He finally asked, rather timidly and afraid.

"I'll explain that to you very soon."

"What type of help do you need from me?"

"It's a very long story, but let me cut it short. I believe that you know about Nidal?"

"Of course, who will not know him? In this area anyone who claims not to know about him has to be dumb. Anyway what is it about him?"

"I am after him and I am out to seek for some information on him."

"In that case you must have come to the wrong place. The only thing that I know about him is that he could be anywhere."

"I know that. The plan is this: Nidal has a training school in Dambatta and I have just graduated from there. They had given us an assignment and I have come with three other men. Our assignment is to take out your camp and kill every soldier here. My three men are outside the camp. Anyway I got into the school as a secret agent trying to get as close to him as possible. The help that I need from you is for you and your men to start shooting into the air and run away so that I can burn down the camp with my men."

"That sounds crazy."

"Yes it is."

"Then why that plan?"

What I will like you to realize is that I want them to see me as a very good terrorist fighter that is loyal to them and in that way I might be able to get some useful information from them. I have no intentions of killing any of you. The training school belongs to Nidal and they are always in contact with him but they always manage to keep every information about him very secret and it is available to only a few of them. I do not want to harm any of you and I would like this conversation to remain a secret between two of us only."

"It is all now beginning to make a lot of sense, but who exactly are you?"

"As a secret agent I will not tell you everything. All I can say for now is that if you can get your bosses to contact the secretary general of your organization, he will surely be able to figure out who I am and what I am doing here. He does not have a hand in what I am doing but he knows all about it. For now I have not contacted anyone, not even my own people, but if you tell him about this incident, he will surely know what to do."

"I will do as you have asked."

"Please try to find a way of contacting him so that it will remain a secret without involving others. At least that way I will still have that advantage of remaining *in cognito* for a little bit longer."As for your immediate boss you can always tell him that a vast army overran the post and that you just managed to bring out all your men alive. We shall do enough to confirm that."

The commandant sat there for a few minutes without Agnes staring embarrassingly at him. Then suddenly he sat straight upright and asked:

"When do you want us to scamper?"

"If possible right away."

"Let's see how I can get them to do that."

"It's very easy. My signal to my men was a burst of three gunshots. I had asked them to keep under cover and fire away into the air without telling them why. I only told them that it was going to be the first step in our line of attack. I have also planted some explosives on all the four cardinal corners of the camp. I will detonate them as you leave and that will help to cement the idea that it was a very large army that overcame you."

"It seems that you had it all planned out before you came in."

"I did."

"Give the signal then, and leave the rest to me."

When Maliki got outside he sent a bunch of three shots from Agnes into the air. His boys started right away to fire into the air and it was at that very moment that he set off his explosives. The commandant was outside already shouting at his men to run down the hill into the town. They only managed to make it into their truck before the last explosion and they did not have to be told to get moving. They drove like mad towards the west and into town. As for Maliki, he systematically took out the tents and burnt them down. He finally called on his men to come out so that he could show them what they had achieved. They were very excited at having achieved so much in their very first assignment. The entire camp had been burnt down and there was one vehicle and one armored personnel carrier that were still ablaze. It was a welcome sight, but he had other plans up his sleeve.

Whenever conditions were not exactly perfect for Agnes he would help her out. One of his men was already way off breezing through the camp in excitement and he felt that it might be best to start with him. He was a little bit too far away for Agnes and so it was his duty to direct her. He could easily bolt away if he started to act and so he had to take him off first. He was not going to leave any loose ends lying about. The man was moving very fast and it was in a zigzag manner. He was almost a hundred yards away or maybe a little more than that. He was not too far away from the outer perimeter of the camp and he could very easily get lost into the surrounding scrubland. He was too far away, he was a moving target and worse still the wind had picked up.

Maliki took into consideration all these and other conditions that could affect the accuracy of a gun. The air was humid and the temperature was high. Agnes for now was using a snub nosed bullet, which was not there for speed and penetration but for maximum damage. He therefore let her aim to a point some four inches above the man's head and three inches off to the left. Agnes was a concept pistol that was built with the full capabilities and strength of a rifle. He therefore switched her to "R' and pulled the hair trigger. As the bullet took flight the force of gravity made it drop downwards but that four inches above the head compensated for that with the distance. The wind had pushed it to the right but that effect was once more cancelled out by that off target aim. Because of the bullets well-balanced center of gravity together with its concurrent protective copper rings, it spun through the air and this minimized any untoward deflection. The final result was that the slug hit the bull's eye. By all means this was an exceptional shot that had been delivered with deadly accuracy.

He was an accomplished sharp shooter. He was a professional shootist. Above all these, he was a celebrated instinctive shooter. All those manipulations and calculations for Agnes had taken but the fraction of a second. All those deadly adjustments had been instantaneously made by instinct as the bullet gained entrance into the man through the center of one ear and exited from the other.

It was obvious that the man had made an irrevocable covenant with death and an agreement with hell sealed with all his dubious and evil ways. A niche must have been reserved for him somewhere in hell. This was probably going to be one of the most turbulent and fiery corners of that infernal furnace. His final moments had come and he did sprint to brace that winners tape from where he was going to join the generation of his fathers. He died but his corpse kept running unawares of the fact that its soul had already raced ahead of it in that journey and race of no return.

He had died on the move as it were, and it was only that initial momentum with which he had taken off that kept him going. He finally slammed into a nearby tree trunk by the roadside and collapsed. He was there as an unsightly lifeless heap and he was sprawled in an awkward position on the ground.

He shot the one who was very close to him and while the other was still puzzled he went into action. As they came closer towards him, still confused but eager to find out what was happening, he wheeled round and back flipped into the air landing behind him. He landed on one leg, but the other leg was on its own personal mission. It delivered a ninja mule kick to the nape of his neck. His neck bone shattered right away severing his spinal cord. The effect of this was to isolate his head from the rest of his body. He was dead right on his feet. His brain was still wondering as to what was going on despite the fact that his body was already on its way to the ground dancing the jitterbug. Rigor mortis could never be better. It was at this instance that he realized that another militant had been sent out to shadow him.

While still delivering that kick, Agnes was still out looking the other way. The remaining militant, that shadow, had just caught a bullet in his chest from a diving shot while he was still in the air. He did not want to take any chances since the man still had a gun with him. The bullet had approached at such an angle and trajectory that after it had passed cleanly through the heart from in-between two ribs it hit the vertebral column behind. It went through one of his intervertebral discs to cut off his spinal cord. It finally got wedged in one of the vertebrae itself. It was the thirteenth to be precise. It turned out to be his unlucky number and so he passed on, not even wiser in any way as to what was going on.

Maliki returned to base in the wee hours of the morning to give his report. The raid was successful but he was the only survivor. He had lost his three colleagues in the fray of the fierce battle together with all the observers.

The camp had been razed to the ground together with quite a bit of hardware. He was sure that their backup would soon be there to attend to the dead.

He was congratulated for a job well done. The dead were not even part of their thoughts; after all they were all expendable. They were essentially of no consequence once they are gone. That was the way and life of the terrorists. Maliki was given three days off before it would be time for him to be re-commissioned. He was to be re-commissioned by none other than Nidal himself. He was already nursing the idea of taking him out there whenever he came in. Nidal had always remained and lived a life that made him seem to be nothing but a phantom. He was like that elusive figment of the imagination that one could not associate with being tangible. Maliki thought that this was going to be an opportunity to end that myth once and for all. This man was more like the proverbial cat with nine lives only that he had much more than nine lives in his own case.

Maliki spent his next few days off inside the bush trying to catch up with some alcohol. He had a cache of Vodka carefully hidden some two feet underground near a tree, which he used as a marker. He had covered his cache with some dried grass to make it look like any other patch of land in that area. He could usually locate it using a few co-ordinates that he had in his head. The vodka was patiently awaiting him but he could not reciprocate. He had gone for vodka so that it would not be easy for anyone in the school to realize that he had been drinking.

The long and short story of the re-commissioning was that Nidal, remaining true to prediction, did not show up. Instead he sent a recorded video message in which he congratulated the school for the success of the assignment and particularly Maliki for his prowess. He was talking of that assignment. He however got another idea after this disappointment. If this elusive character was able to send a message to them, then their office, which incidentally was always under lock and key, must know how to get to him. These people were a little bit too smart. They had computers in the front office but there was no useful information in them. During one of their lessons on computer usage he had tried to hack into their database. It seems that they were aware of the fact that computers were there only to keep secrets as open secrets and so they had to rely on paper work. The paper documents must be somewhere behind that locked door and he planned to get to them one way or the other.

That very night Maliki went into action. He stole his way to the office building and gained entrance into it through one small window at the back. He got straight into the inner room. It was a very small room with just one table and a chair. The rest was just one big metal walk in safe. It took him the better half of fifteen minutes to pick the lock of the safe with the help of his penlight. The safe was neatly stacked with crisp currencies but he was not interested in that. His eyes eventually caught what he felt would be of interest to him and that was a few files.

They were just three manila files that were held together with the aid of a rubber band and tucked away in one corner. He quickly retrieved them and scanned through them. There was nothing outstanding or of any particular interest about them. They were mainly the common day-to-day interoffice memos. Then suddenly the clue he was after came to him.

Most of the letters were posted from different countries and all the memos were from Nidal. He therefore copied down the towns and zip codes that they were posted from. They came from six different countries. The implication of this find is that if he went to these different zip codes he would be very close to him or at least to his contact in each of them. Home to Nidal could be a cave or anything that could house a man. He was a man vowed to frugality. When he came out of the office he made it straight into the town to collect the rest of his gear before coming back to the school. At the school he informed them that he was not feeling too well and so he wanted to spend the next three days out of sight in a room in the town. It was, according to him, something that he used to do whenever he needed to meditate for supreme guidance in his actions. He explained that he was going to come back to action and they were excited about that. What they did not however realize is that he was off to hunt for their leader.

Nidal was a very sly and crafty character and Abu Maliki was very much aware of that. He was for sure equal to the task and now he had that advantage of surprise. He was going to hit fast otherwise they might have the opportunity to dodge. Once he starts there was not going to be any looking back and he had to get to the end before stopping. He had been trained in and around Dambatta twice now and he knew what to expect. Dambatta was not in good relations with Aridopolis their neighboring country, and that was where the United Nations troops had run into. Nidal, of all places, also had a base right there in Aridopolis. No one would have expected that. Aridipolis was a completely desert country and there was a very high mountain range there. The top of the mountain range was completely inaccessible to people due to very dangerous and deadly terrains, but Nidal had his base right on top of that range. One of his letters had come from Aridopolis and it was addressed from a unit there. That was his research and production outfit. He had "built" a monastery there and no one was sure of which order that monastery belonged to, but it was there. About thirty reclusive hermits inhabited it and none of them had ever been sighted in well over ten years. Nidal had wiped out the original Coptic sect occupants and converted the place to his base. It was mainly accessible only from the air but for him and his group of hermits it had to be by foot and that was impossible. In short once there none could ever come out except for himself who often used a motorized glider to get in and out of there once in a while. These were usually done at night when there were no eyes to witness that.

The school at Dambatta knew that they were preparing to test a new weapon and that was the reason for the eagerness for their hero to hang around. Nidal wanted to test this new weapon and that was why he wanted the two countries to fight so that the opportunity would present itself for him to step in. This was the reason for the United Nations outpost destruction. All the observers had been flown out of the country for the mean time.

As Maliki was to find out later, his quarry had a very devious mind, more devious than he had ever imagined. He was going to arm his militants in Dambatta to help that country to overrun Aridopolis. Even when Aridopolis is defeated he would be safe up in his mountain fortress. Aridopolis was a much larger and better-equipped nation and they were no match for each other. He was however going to help Dambatta to win the war.

Maliki therefore found himself back in the school, as part of his plans, to help Dambatta in the war. He was there as a mercenary contracted as an independent private contractor to help with the war. As an independent contractor, Maliki had agreed to invade Aridopolis on behalf of Dambatta. That very evening a tank arrived from Nidal. It was carried into the school compound on a low loader trailer, tightly covered and secured to the vehicle.

Around five in the morning they were all called out

to be introduced to the vehicle. It was about the size of a very large truck and it cost well over a billion dollars to produce. Its body was of an unknown titanium alloy, which made it very light but totally impenetrable by any ammunition or ordinance. It was bullet proof, it was immune to every known type of warhead and it was explosion proof. Even a blow touch would not as much as succeed to give it a scratch. It was the child of the ADELA technological institute.

Despite this outer formidable and impenetrable casing, the tank was equipped with something that was comparatively very sinister. In the place of shells it was able to shoot out tiny cruise missiles each of which had a range of at least two hundred miles. They were guided from within the tank and they were of the hell fire group of missiles. To make matters worse they were capable of carrying nuclear warheads and no one could be sure of which it was armed with at any given moment. It could be conventional and it could be nuclear. This meant that they could easily send cruise missiles at well below the radar detecting height and take out targets that are two hundred miles away with pinpoint accuracy. Each of these tiny bombs would be capable of one-mile radius physical destruction. Maliki was not going to let this happen.

Again some of these missiles had antiaircraft capabilities. They are usually shot off from the tank at about MACH one speed but this is so only till they engage their own short lived propulsion mechanisms. This would be able to take them to speeds in excess of MACH three. No warplane could therefore ever out -fly or escape any of them. For the attack on Aridopolis they were going to use only conventional warheads. The government of Dambatta had agreed to pay for all these and more.

This tank was more complicated than it was unique. Two resident evils lived inside the tank. These were two well-trained Orang- Otangs and their handler. They were trained to be able to detect and dodge land mines and they were each trained to blow themselves up together with whatever they found at their destinations. They were apes and so they could scale any walls with ease and so they were the first to enter any camp. For this particular mission they were armed with grenades. At first they were introduced to take over from the tanks whenever they got to any impenetrable forests where they would be at home.

It was going to be an unprovoked pre-emptive strike and they had just another twelve hours to get ready. Maliki was chosen as the leader of this elite strike force. There were only six men in the unit – an extremely small but very effective unit. He was given a geographical map and topographical layout of the city so that he could be at home with the place for the attack. He familiarized himself with everything as instructed, but he also made sure of how to trace the mountaintop from there.

While this was going on, Maliki had called the secretary of state at home. He was to deliver some one hundred non-destructive explosives to a predetermined site around the razed United Nations camp. It was a very urgent request and they were sent there within five hours through the new United Nations peacekeeping forces. They were delivered in a particular specified size and shape and they were the type used in fireworks.

The attack was going to be by night, and that razed down United Nations camp was going to be their launching pad.

The Armageddon ET1 tank, as it was called, was driven by Maliki himself. He had got a lot of information and he was ready for action. It is claimed that thunder does not usually strike twice on the same spot, but this time around it was going to do so. He also arranged for the school at the base of the hill to the rendezvous to go into assembly and hold an all night prayers for them before they set off as well as while they were there. Their work was to destroy the city and come right back to the school. The entire force was made up of himself, two other militants, Tim and Timothy – those two Orang-Otangs and then their trainer.

When they got to their staging ground, Maliki positioned the tank at the center of the previous United Nations camp. One luck he had was that in the military services, no matter how crude or which type, it was customary for one to obey his officer first and then ask questions later. He ordered the men to go down to the school to collect some things that they had left behind by mistake. As soon as he could sight them with his binoculars inside the school compound he let fly one of the missiles. The school was razed to the ground and only he and the apes were left to continue with the raid. The organization had therefore lost its school together with all the recruits and trainers. It was a big blow. He then retrieved those blank explosives and then loaded them into the tank. With these he made a lot of noise shooting all over Aridopolis.

He would have tried to take out the monastery from there but he finally decided to wait and try to find out what was inside there first. Maliki had arranged for his home country to send some soldiers to that camp, and by the time they got there, that tank was waiting for them. That was the Armageddon End Times Tank model one, for that was its full name. They were to pick up the tank and he had left some operational instructions in it for them, but that was not before he had let Agnes take out those two apes. It was eventually a Hercules C- twenty transport aircraft that was employed to fly it home.

Maliki was off to the monastery.

It was a long and difficult journey for Maliki as he tried to make it up to the monastery. It was on the very top of the mountains, which seemed to be right inside the skies. He did the first leg of the journey in a car and then continued on a motorcycle. Unlike the rest of the country, this terrain was totally unforgiving and it was different. Somehow or the other, or for quite some inexplicable reasons, the vegetation seemed to increase with the height. The lower expanse was mainly of rocks and boulders with sandy tracks in-between. It soon became obvious that the mountain had defeated his motorcycle and so he abandoned it by one shrub and continued on foot. The incline had become too steep for any motorized vehicle but his feet were well seasoned and equal to the task. There were occasional boulders, many of them precariously and treacherously perched as he went further up, but this was not the type of time for one to give up. With time he was within hearing distance of the monastery and he could very easily see it perched on top of one of the pinnacles. It was probably one of those rocky outcrops of an extinct volcano.

The entire topography tended to tell its own different story. It tended to indicate that there must have been an earthquake around here sometime in the distant past. Maybe this was what broke off all those boulders from the mountainsides that were strewn all over the place. Some of these were as large as, if not larger than houses. The weather through erosions and denudation must have added their own, but he had finally conquered that treacherous terrain.

By the time he got to the last stretch it had changed to a sheer rocky cliff. It was as good as impossible to climb, but footholds had been chiseled out of the rock for ardent climbers. There were definitely none to do so. Maliki was equal to the task and he made an effort to do so. There was a lone owl that was hooting just outside the wall and it stopped when it saw him. It looked as if they were the only living things within the vicinity of that cliff. The outside walls of the monastery were not very high on their own. They did not seem to have been built to keep away intruders but rather to prevent the inmates from falling down the cliff. He waited a little bit to observe what was going on before climbing over it in the darkness. The air up there was very thin and with the deepening night towards dawn, it was also getting crispier and cold.

It was quite windy up there, and now adding the wind chill to the low temperature, up it was obvious why the people who lived there go in so early and sleep till late. There were four buildings there and he took his time to sneak around each to find out its exact layout and probably use too. The smallest building was also the tallest and it must have been a chapel long ago. Now it seems to be used as a research laboratory. He could see through the windows into the dim rooms. There were machine tool benches as well as tables with those chemical research paraphernalia. The biggest building was an indoor training hall or gym, but it also had what seemed to be a dining area at the very end of it. The other two buildings were living quarters with one of them serving as an office as well. Whoever ran the place must therefore live there.

He had come fully prepared for whatever situation

that could present itself. He had also planted some explosives outside each of the buildings. These were those miniaturized high incendiary explosives that were his trademark. Each was the size of a short cigarette but packed the punch of over five hundred sticks of dynamite stuck together. He had always had these as his signature since his days with the secret service, and he was able to lay his hands on these because of his usefulness to the government. He estimated that there were going to be about a hundred and fifty inhabitants in the place. Nidal was probably not there since the few people he had sighted inside did not seem to be on the edge which should have been the case if their boss was around. They looked too relaxed.

He wanted to find out more and for that reason he was not going to destroy the place right away. He gained entrance into the office through the window and began to search for any new clues as to how to locate Nidal. There were three rooms there. Two of the rooms were used as warehouses but the third was a bare room, which was how he figured that the main office would look like. He went in there and pried open all the table drawers that he came across. As usual one of them contained files, which were what he was after. They were just like the previous files that he had come across in Dambatta, each full of memos, but one had an enlightening entry. Nidal left the base just a day earlier for Chatanuga

Chatanuga was of course going to be his next port of

call. Things then took a different turn as a man suddenly stepped into the office. He had to change his plans. This man was the office guard and he seemed to live in the next room. He probably heard some noise and decided to investigate. This man must have been very much on the alert because he had made every effort to be as quiet as possible as he went about his business. The man had come in equally quiet too.

The lights were suddenly flicked on and Maliki went blind but for an instant. The guard did not expect to see him there and so he was too surprised to take immediate action or at least take advantage of the effects of that light. That gave Maliki the opportunity to recover. The man was simply just as big as it could get. He was almost eight feet tall and very huge and his face was as scary as it could get. Maliki did not want to waste any time and so he immediately went into action. He knelt down and put his hands together and began to pray for his safety and leniency in Urdu. The big man was too surprised at the turn of events. He could not understand one single word that the man spoke, but the gesticulations were evidence that he was pleading for mercy. He had a gun in his hand but all the same he got a little bit closer to take a better look of the intruder.

It was then that Maliki made his move. It was a fast flying dive with his head aimed straight for the man's groins. His head connected and the man did exactly what he was expected to do. He staggered backwards, dropped his gun and then tried to grab and protect his aching groins with both hands. Maliki had fallen to the ground with both hands on the ground in front of him as if he were getting ready for the pushups. With both hands, as both support and fulcrum, he arched his body backwards as his ankles flew up and wound around the big man's neck in an evertightenning foot strangle grip. Eventually he flung his body erect and grabbed on to a ceiling beam. With this as support he squeezed harder on the neck till the man let his groins alone and started trying to pry loose his ankles in an attempt to let in more air into his lungs. It was however a fruitless effort.

Just as he was gasping for his last breathe, his vertebrae snapped. He therefore left without any more fanfare. As Maliki let go of the now limp body, a second guard dashed in, probably from the outermost room. He must have heard the noise of the fighting. Maliki was ready this time around. He did not let him have enough time to absorb the situation or to sympathize with his colleague before he let out a serial sidekick towards him. He hopped on one leg before letting the other one lash out sideways at an incredible speed. It was able to deliver incredibly strong serial kicks to the side of his head at a rate not far from four hits per second. That was enough to drop the man to the floor with blood already beginning to sip out of the corners of his mouth. He had died without knowing exactly what had happened to him. One of the kicks had done in his Adams apple.

Maliki meant business and he was not in the mood to waste any time up there since Nidal was not there. He quickly stole back to the ledge and climbed down the mountain. He used his remote control to detonate the explosives from almost a mile down. With that all the buildings in the monastery together with the hoodlums who inhabited it were gone. The boom was heard from all over Aridopolis to far beyond. They all assumed that it must be another earthquake, which were not too infrequent there, or maybe it could be the prelude to a volcanic eruption from the extinct crater.

As soon as he hit town, he was off on his way to Chatanuga.

Chatanuga

His approach to Chatanuga was going to be a fairly tricky one. He was not sure of where the headquarters was, but according to the documents their contact man there was the spiritual leader of the Jobist congregation there. All their letters had come from there too, though it did not make a lot of sense. He only tried to place them as another group of Christians who were in on the deal with Nidal. They could also be another group of monks who were no more. Chatanuga was a landlocked nation but it was famous for being the world's largest producer of iron ore. Cherryville was the town from where all the letters were postmarked and so he headed straight for there. It was also the capital of Chatanuga. As providence would have it, the man who sat next to him during the flight to Chatanuga turned out to be a person of interest. He was the self-proclaimed high priest of the order of the Jobists as he put it. They had introduced themselves to each other as they sat in the first class section of the plane.

He was a big and apparently unpretentious gentleman.

When the hostess came to serve them, the man demanded for shitake mushrooms and nothing else. He did not want meat and he did not want any green vegetables either. The hostess explained that shitake mushrooms were usually included in their menu as a la carte, but the man insisted that they knew that he was in the plane and so they should have had it included in their menu. He was a regular customer and so he felt that they should have been aware of that. The hostess then explained that he came in without any previous booking just a few minutes before the flight and that was why they had no time to get something for him. That explanation only fell on deaf ears and so Maliki stepped in:

"Excuse me sir?"

"How can I help you?" He snapped back at Maliki.

"I am sorry if I have offended you, but I was only trying to see if there is any way that I could be of help."

"I am very sorry, but there is no way that you can help."

"But I happen to have a can of shitake mushrooms in my bag." Ike had come to make this his favorite snack because it was claimed to contain a lot of chemicals that helped to boost the immune system.

"And so what?"

"Would you like me to give it to her to prepare for you since I have no immediate need for it?"

"You'll do that?"

"Yes."

"No, don't worry yourself on my behalf and thanks for that offer."

"But we still have another twelve hours to go and you might need something to eat before the flight is over."

"I am aware of that, but as a priest I can always go into a fast and so that does not really matter."

"Ok then. I hope you don't mind my curiosity. Why don't you want to eat any other thing?"

"It has to do with my religious beliefs and practices."

"Which religion is that?"

"Have you ever heard of the Jobists?"

"No. But my guess is that you must be a Christian group?"

"You are not too far from the truth with that assumption. However we are not exactly Christians, but we use the holy bible as our canon. Unlike the Christians however we tend to oppose some of its teachings."

"How could it be your holy book if you don't agree with many things in it?"

"Christians use it because they want to believe everything in it and that is how they get their own inspiration. In our own case we get our own inspiration at times by going against it. In short we try to be philosophical about the whole thing. Moreover we are not hypocrites. Many of the Christians tell you that they believe in it and yet they would go against it without owning up that they are doing so."

"I am not too sure of that."

"There are many instances where they choose what they want over the teachings of the bible. For instance, it asked that though women could teach other women they should not teach in a way as to be the head of the churches. Well they are even bishops. Same sex relationships are even punishable by death, but they are not just condoned but are even bishops. The list is rather very long."

"What you say is true."

"Not too many people can see with us that fast."

"When it comes to religion, I have always had an open mind."

"I can see that."

"If I may ask; how did you come by that name that you use?"

"If you go through the book of Job in the bible the first thing that will occur to you is Jobs attitude. He spent most of his time arguing with God and demanding explanations for situations around which he felt that God created which did not seem right to him. He was very close to God. It is therefore imperative that there are various ways to follow god. Job demanded explanations while Abraham followed without questioning and with faith. Like the Christians, the truthful ones that is, Abraham obeyed through faith. We are like Job."

"I am beginning to see more and more with your line of argument."

"Once more do not forget that even Thomas went right ahead to doubt his own master whom he knew personally.

Who are we therefore not to doubt too. Explanations and evidence seem to be the right way."

If not for what you have been saying I would have thought that to doubt God in any way at all would not just be unacceptable but will be blasphemy. Now I seem to see it differently, though to serve him with faith seems to have been one of his injunctions."

"You are right there. All we are saying is that there are many ways, and it is for us to choose one of them"

"I completely agree with you."

"Many people make that mistake of thinking that there is only one way."

Ike was aware of the fact that whoever this man was, he could be connected with his contact if he is not the person. He therefore decided to exploit the situation further:

"Do you have a church there that you run?"

"Yes, and I can see that this is your first visit to Cherryville."

"Yes and I am just a tourist."

"Do you have any contact there?"

"No, but I was booked into the Darby Manor inn."

"That's a nice little hotel and it is not too far from me. I happen to be the chief priest of the Jobists and our church is only about three hundred yards away from that inn."

"What a coincidence!"

"Feel free to visit us. You are invited."

"I will be there."

"I actually came here because I used to be an archeologist. I have retired now but when I was told that there are a lot of underground caverns in these areas I decided to vacation around here. The idea is to explore some of the caves and caverns."

"You are absolutely right. Iron mining created most of the caverns. They are mainly abandoned underground mines."

"How safe are they?"

"They are quite safe and there are tourist guides all over."

"I can't wait to explore the place."

"What else do you do for a living?"

"Beyond archeology, I used to be a soldier, but nowadays I only fight on demand, if you know what I mean."

"A mercenary?"

"Not exactly. I am more like a free lance militant ready to be hired out for a fee."

"What a coincidence. Why don't you make out time to see me whenever you have rested? I might be able to link you up with someone who might be interested in you."

"That would be great. It seems that I cannot wait to get there."

"What experience do you have in fighting?"

"I have fought for about three countries, the united nations and some militant groups."

"I guess it's time for a little nap. Please don't forget to

look me up when we get there. Just come to the church and tell them that you want to have an audience with the chief priest. My name is Thomas Job."

"I will do so and thanks again."

He was on the right track!

As soon as they landed at the Cherryville airport, Maliki left for his inn in an airport taxi. It was already getting dark but he did not fail to notice that Job left in a limo that seemed to have been there waiting for him. He had chosen that inn because it had the same zip code as was on the letters at the office in the monastery. He then decided to sleep before making a survey of the entire area in the morning. He was however in for a very pleasant surprise in the morning. The Jobist's church was less than a hundred yards away from the inn and they were both within that very same zip code. Does it mean that Nidal operated from that church? No. It was not possible; at least the place was too open for him. Maybe he could get closer to the truth by going there. His best alternative was therefore to take up that offer from the chief priest.

He therefore went to the church a little bit later. Once inside it was easy to locate the office to the chief priest. He introduced himself to the chief priest's secretary who informed him that Job had to travel out on an emergency but that he might be back that very evening. He however tried to pry out one information or the other from the man after he had asked for his exact contact information.

"Is there any message that I could leave for him when he returns?" The man asked.

"Just tell him that Maliki was here. I am the man that he met in the plane."

"When was that?"

"Yesterday."

"From Aridopolis?"

"Yes."

"Any other message?"

"Nothing really. It is just that we discussed some prospects of work."

"Actually I am not just his secretary. I am his personal assistant as well as his second in command. I am reverend Moses and I can always help with any problems.

"I didn't know that; maybe you could actually be of help."

"What type of work were you looking for?"

"He promised to get me in contact with someone who might need some free lance soldiers."

"And what are your experiences in that line?"

Maliki then went ahead to recant the same story that he had told Job before he was made to answer a few questions as to his identity. He knew that they would like to make sure that he was not a spy or something like that. On his part he wanted to be in a hurry. Maybe Job came in before he got news of the monastery and that must be why he had to leave so soon. Moses finally asked him to come in early in the morning so that he could get that very potential employer to the church. He thanked him and left fully aware of the fact that he was on the right track.

When he came to the church the following morning Job was there. According to Job, the contractor had asked him to interview the candidate for him. The assignment was to blow out the unity central train station right there in Cherryville. He accepted the offer for the specified fee. Finally Job decided to let him in on a surprise now that he had become a close associate of theirs.

He was led through the church to the altar. The altar had a very high canopy, which was made of lightly colored translucent tiles. This was able to let in light in a dazzling as well as dizzying kaleidoscopic manner. It was essentially like a fantastic celebration to the eyes. It even becomes more apparent, more mesmerizing and most attention catching with the passing of the clouds. This meant that with the dying hours of each day, as the sun fades into the west, the same was going to happen. This would be when the moon would be rearing up her head impatiently in an attempt to take over the rulership of the darkening skies from the sun. There was a shelf there with a couple of gold chalices and Job reached behind one of the chalices and pressed a button. The Eucharistic table immediately swung to one side and a trap door opened on its own from beneath it.

They went down a flight of stairs into a dimly lit passage and then from there into a very big hall. This must have been more than a hundred feet below the ground level. Many other passages branched off this hall, but they were all dark. The hall was very large, as well as high, and there were about thirty men there training. This must be an underground school. All the pieces of the puzzle were now beginning to fall into place. This was the base he had in mind. Nidal was surely the owner of the place.

For some inexplicable reason Maliki had been accepted as one of them. Job had explained to him that they were in an abandoned iron ore mine. They had sealed off that area for their own use. The dark passages that he saw led to smaller storage rooms. It was from here that they directed all their operations. Job was the boss for this organization and they were there as an agency for violent opposition to the government. In short they were a terrorist organization. The only thing left for Maliki was to see the link to Nidal.

Job had taken Maliki down there to introduce him to their activities with the hope that he was going to be one of his tools for his nefarious activities. Job was however not aware of the fact that he was only inviting that grim reaper to his base, and this agent had other plans for him. These people had invested in corruption and violence, and though they might seem to be profitable ventures, which they were, the end is not always good. Death was going to use Maliki to reap a few more souls from his fold. Maliki was there and very much on the alert. Agnes was also there and in the same mood too. She was for now very comfortably nestled in her well-oiled chamois leather holster beneath his jacket between his left arm and his body. She was fully pregnant with bullets and essentially in labor.

Maliki knew what he was supposed to do. Nidal was not there but he intended to hunt him from one hiding place to the other till he catches up with him. For now he had to do what he had to do. He had to interrupt Job halfway through his introduction to his men in the gym with the question;

"Can I ask you one funny question Reverend Job?"

"Sure enough. Go right ahead."

"Are you per chance very familiar with that training school at Dambatta?"

"I believe that I have heard of it, but why do you ask?"

Maliki was watching his reaction and he did not fail to notice that he flinched ever so imperceptibly to that unexpected question.

"Are you aware of the fact that the school is no more?"

"I just heard that a few moments ago in the news, but once more why do you have to ask that question?"

"I was the person who took it out."

"What do you mean by that?"

His voice had changed a little bit and there was a little bit of that edge of concern to it.

"What of Nidal?"

"Who is Nidal?"

"I guess I have to take you out too since you don't know him. You might not be of any use to me." With that he flashed out Agnes who sprang into his right hand. She had come out as he twirled and tried to reach under his jacket. The whole thing happened so fast that it seemed to have been just a blur. Both the speed with which she came out, the unexpectedness of her appearance and the dexterity with which her trigger balanced just beneath his index finger puzzled everyone around. Unfortunately for them, but fortunately for him, guns were not usually allowed down there.

Before he could complete the spin, Agnes had let out two hurried and impatient bullets. The first got Job on the left side of his chest and passed through his heart to let out bright red blood. The second one came only a split second later but it went through his mouth. It was this second one that actually did more damage than the first. Following a geometrical trajectory and with trigonometrical precision, it had gone through an interesting adventure. It passed through the mouth shattering four of his teeth and these tried to force their way down his throat. They nearly choked him. It then travelled through his upper palate to his brain, lingering for a little while within his medulla oblongata. It was for maybe less than a nanosecond, but that hesitancy was enough to paralyze his sensory systems. It however continued to ricochet off the back of his skull where he had a metal plate put in during a past surgery and churned its way backwards. It passed through the cerebrum and cerebellum and that rendered his entire brain useless. It had been essentially mashed up and he was dead long before he could have had the opportunity to realize what was happening.

Before Agnes, who was now spinning in his palm, could complete one spin she had sent another bullet into Moses. It went right through the center of his forehead between his eyes and he was gone to give an account of his stewardship here on earth to his maker. He was surely not going to receive a positive report. As a reverend gentleman he was going too be judged on a higher standard than the rest.

Agnes was his first line of action and the men in the arena fell like ninepins in a bowling alley. Many more fell as he quickly changed her clips. By the time that she was done there were only a few of them left. Maliki had no time to explain anything to any of them and he did not actually have any time to waste. They had all been trained to destroy, and most of them were going to be suicide bombers, and so eliminating them would be doing a lot of service to the human race. He therefore fell on them using whichever technique came first.

The first man to fall left with a sizzling karate chop to his temple. He was not just dazzled but his brain received such a jolt that he died from the shock of it all. The next two were dispatched with a double sided or twin decapitator kick. He had jumped into the air between the two of them with each leg lashing out violently sideways. Each took down its target and they both met their ends without even the slightest protest.

The next man dared an overambitious maneuver, which brought him too close to his nemesis. He came with a lot of irrelevant and ineffective thrash talk and rants. This was an attempt to psyche out Maliki, but he only succeeded in annoying him. He also lost some concentration with that and that cost him his life. A clandestine adjudicative tornado kick, as it was called in the school of martial arts, was what settled the case. The issue at hand was more of how he was going to die than whether he was going to live or die. It was already obvious that he was going to die. It was a more deadly variant of the jugular kick. It simply ripped off his Adams apple while occluding his jugular veins with pressure that was strong enough to plaster them against his own bones. He was in so much of a hurry to die that he could not even wait for the pain to radiate through his body before he gave up the ghost. His remains settled down in a pool of his own blood.

One of them tried to sneak by him into one of those dark passages, but it was already too late for him by the time he got to where he was. Maliki back-flipped in such a manner that the man who had essentially got to safety suddenly found himself standing face to face with him. That particular passage was now right between the two of them but nearer to Maliki. He was too confused as to what to do next and so he knelt down to plead for mercy. That was of course not a viable option under these situations.

Maliki simply delivered him onto his maker with a vicious whirlwind kung fu blow to his chest. That was enough to crack most of his thoracic ribs on the left side with their pieces macerated with his heart in an instant. He died long before his corpse could hit the floor.

The remaining one was a little bit wiser than the rest. He pleaded for mercy in exchange for information. All that Maliki wanted to know was when Nidal came there last and where he was headed. The man claimed that he was there more than a month earlier and also that rumor had it that he died in a missile attack on the Dambatta training school just a few days earlier.

Maliki felt that the information did not agree with what he did and what he knew, and so it was obvious that the man had just insulted his intelligence. What he said was false and so he had to take him out with fury. He took a lunge at the man and his head connected to his torso. The man fell backwards as his breath left him with a gentle but ever fading swish in a final lullaby as he lapsed into eternal sleep. To finally dissipate his fury he still jumped into the air and came down on the man's throat with his legs together. The idiot whom he thought was already dead was recalled but for a fleeting instance to dance his farewell jitterbug.

It was claimed in an adage that when a dog begins to near its death, it will forget the smell and enticing odor of bones. One idiot who was probably their storekeeper, despite having witnessed what had happened, stumbled out of one of those dark passages. He made a halfhearted attempt to fight Maliki. He was a dithering and reluctant fighter who was definitely feeble minded. His efforts were essentially inconsequential. As soon as his feeble mind came to and he remembered what he had seen before, he fell ill. Maliki tried to imagine an electroencephalogram being attached to the man. He was sure that the electroencephalograph that would be produced by this was bound to be full of abnormal spikes. He then suddenly seemed to turn cataleptic, and before Maliki could make any moves he was gone. It was his end and he had died without as much as a single blow. He had cheated Maliki out of a fight, but then every cloud had its own silver lining. The man had just saved him valuable time, as he had to be on his way. Any second saved was going to be important and so he was not annoyed at the man.

He was not the last man standing anyway. Someone had just climbed down the stairs as he made his way back. The man must have witnessed his last actions and commiseration nearly took hold of him when he realized that the man had been stricken stiff with fear. To make matters worse he had just wetted his pants. He succumbed to that sympathetic sight and did just what any other gentleman would do under such dire circumstances. He quickly relieved the man of his fears and snapped him out of his stupor. It was a very simple process. He used the butt of his gun Agnes to deliver a home coming blow to the man's fontanel and that did the trick. He however died without thanking him for his kindness as would be expected. His soul had unapologetically left for Hades. It left secretly and in a hurry on AWOL, Away Without Official Leave, and his destination was hell. This was one of those classical situations where the climate of hell would be better and more comfortable than life itself on earth. For him it was the better of the two alternatives.

To seal the entire deal with his signature, he left two explosives there. One was at the center of the hall and the other at the trap door. This was however after he had gone into the office to seek some more information.

According to the most recent entries in their books, Nidal passed through there two days earlier on his way for a convention in EMOR. The convention was just for one day and so it should have been over. Be that as it may, it was obvious that the next step to take had to be to get to EMOR.

Maliki was officially asleep in his room in the inn when the explosions took place. He had detonated the two explosives only after he had got home. The one in the hall caused a mild but comparatively localized earthquake, while the one near the altar brought down the Jobist's church. The rubbles buried all the secrets with the dead. It was going to be for archeologists to take a guess at what had happened – maybe right, maybe wrong. No one knew that people lived underground there and so no one would miss them. More importantly however is the fact that earthquakes were not too infrequent there. Those inhabitants of the underground there had always yearned to remain anonymous and so even at death their wishes had been granted. They were not missed by anyone, and they had achieved anonymity.

Those explosions had reenacted the incidences that went with Mount Vesuvius on Pompeii, but this time around it was a little bit more localized. Those underground crypts and caverns had been preserved for eternity and for people to ponder at in the future. It had turned into a burial chamber for a lot of Nidal's men and apostles. The entire labyrinthine maze of passages in the area had gone down to be preserved as history for those prying eyes of meddling archeologists. Only wrong educated guesses will come to be the truth by then. No one will ever know the actual truth.

That very evening Maliki was off to the airport for a transcontinental flight to EMOR.

From Emor to Intipuga

EMOR was an ancient country with its capital Emoreville claimed to be one of the oldest continuously inhabited cities on earth. It nestled comfortably amongst a few hills. Because this city had been continuously inhabited for many centuries, land was a little bit scarce there. They had therefore devised a few ingenious ways to make do with the little land they had. One was to build their houses to be very tall and the other was to utilize the underground.

The transcontinental flight had landed in the Emoreville airport around midnight and Maliki checked into the "Hotel Senorita." This was their airport hotel, and it was an imposing edifice on its own. It was a five star hotel and owned by one "Lady Bianca."

Bianca was one of those society ladies who was used to the various ways to move and shake things around in the town. She was well linked with politicians and she ran the type of business that would always get them whatever they wanted.

Hotel Senorita had several small and discrete conference rooms that were often used by politicians whenever they wanted to meet with lobbyists. In short whenever they wanted to go for discussions or deals that could put them in trouble, they would go down to that hotel. It was a common saying there that, "whatever took place at the Senorita always stayed at the Senorita." This was not the only attraction to this very hotel. She also ran a very sophisticated and discrete call girl and prostitution business from there. She had a lot of live-in call girls who were hardly ever seen in public. They were handpicked and many of them were previous beauty queens or at least previous beauty pageant contestants. She herself was an ex beauty queen and it was rumored that she went into business through the largesse of the contest sponsor.

In other words Bianca herself was a very artfully crafted handwork of nature. She was one of those women who have defied the ages as well as the process of aging. She was one of those curiosities that had that uncanny habit of getting younger as well as prettier with age. In summary, she was ageless and was on occasions described by the grapevine as the ageless beauty.

Some of the girls were actually highly well placed. Many were university students who wanted to make a little money by the side to help supplement their educational expenses. A few were dedicated housewives who came for some fun, especially those whose spouses were in professions that kept them travelling most of the time.

One of them was the wife to an ambassador who was off to serve the country in a foreign country, and a few were soldier's wives. Their husbands were away in action. There were the ones that were simply promiscuous as typified by the professor of mathematics who shared the same room with her daughter who was a surgeon.

This would have been the most unlikely place for Maliki to stay, but he had his reasons. Emoreville was a sin city and Hotel Senorita was the heartthrob of the city. If Nidal was going to be around, it was obvious that he must have something to do with the place. For now he had no single lead towards his quest. The letters that were from there simply came from a post office box and that was all.

When he stepped into the hotel for the first time he did not fail to notice that the bar was well stocked with all sorts of rare vintages. He was attracted to that, but he had to control himself. It was going to be a war of nerves between Ike and Maliki. Maliki however had to win. Ike was a hard drinker, Maliki was a teetotaler, but as for himself as the third factor in this dilemma, he was going to get over them both. He once thought that just one little sip was not going to do him any harm but then his dressing would not be in line with that, and to be seen around the bar in his caftan would be like seeing a fish looking for water out of water. He finally ordered a few bottles for his friends who might come around to visit him. He was eventually the visitor and the only visitor to his room as he did justice to the bottles. He was not convinced that this came as a result of irrepressible gluttony but he took it as just a habit.

On his very first night in the hotel he noticed something very odd which aroused his curiosity. There was a statue of the Madonna, which was just outside a cathedral that was some fifty yards away. From the window of his room he could realize that there was some activity around it. The statue was housed in a small shrine whose front housed the statue while the back was a platform on which people could drop off donations. Around midnight he saw three men step through the slab as if it was not there. Maybe they were ghosts.

Early in the morning he went to the slab and donated ten dollars to the cause of the Madonna. The slab was solid and would not give way under him as it seemed to have done for those men. That very evening he decided to ask one of the girls about that slab. There was this lady who was in the habit of always looking at him. She looked a little bit too sophisticated to be there and he felt that she was definitely out of place, though for this hotel nothing could ever be out of place. A lot of times he would see her browsing through one book or the other in the library, which was by the lobby. He just went in to where she was and started off a conversation:

"Good morning miss."

"Good morning. What can I do for you?"

"Nothing for now. However I am researching into

something and I thought that since you are always around the library you might know something about it."

"What could that be about then?"

"First of all my name is Maliki, and you?"

"Sophia."

"And what do you do here?"

"Just hanging around and watching out for customers. I am a professor of psychology in the university."

"Which university could that be?"

"Saint Dryden's University of Theology."

"I hope you don't mind, I did not quite get what you said you were doing here."

"You seem to be a very inquisitive man."

"Yes I know that, but it is all because of my interest in you."

"Well, I am into the escort business."

"As a professor of psychology, what area did you specialize in?"

"The effects of parapsychic phenomena on individuals."

"Thank God, you are just the person that I need."

"In what way, and what is your mission here?"

"I am a tourist, but last night I witnessed things that I thought were parapsychic phenomena. At first I thought that it was just my imagination, but it was real."

"Where?"

"By the statue of the Madonna near the cathedral late last night."

"Are you sure of that?"

"Yes and I am ready to pay you for the night to come in and stay in my room so that you can observe them first hand."

With that he went ahead to describe what he had witnessed to her. He still wondered how people could disappear through a solid slab of concrete. If she could come in for the night she might be able to see it herself and so explain it to him. After a little more persuasion, Sophia agreed to come over to his room by ten in the night and see what it was that he said happens around midnight.

She came in to his room by ten minutes after ten in the night looking lovelier than she had ever been. They sat together by the window looking out towards the statue of the Madonna as they told each other stories of their experiences. Both she and her daughter had been abused and each was now divorced and it was the trauma of those abuses that led to their current preferences. They each had a pair of night vision binoculars for closer inspection. Around ten minutes to midnight two men came there. They seemed to survey all around before going to that slab behind the statue. They looked on in amazement as the two men vanished underground.

EMOR was a twin city. It had an upper and a lower city. The lower underground city was created the first time they ran short of space. That was when men began to sell the spaces under their houses to others to use in building their own underneath. These were mainly crypts and burial chambers. The underground was however riddled with canals and sewer systems. It eventually developed into a maze of catacombs and many areas had been cordoned off and were actually very large rooms.

According to Sophia, most of the crypts were later sealed off with the introduction of cremation, but most importantly after the great plague it was decided that many had been buried below who were infected. It was the only way that they imagined that could help them keep the plague in check – underground. All the crypts were sealed off except for a few.

The cathedral was known to have a vast crypt where most of their earlier bishops were buried. It was also known to be rich in other religious relics. Once a year select visitors were allowed into it during the "feast of the fallen saints." People were reported to have witnessed a lot of manifestations in various parts of the city, but most were around the cathedral. Sophia was doing her post-doctoral research on these sittings. From all that she had found out so far, these were not manifestations at all. She had investigated one particular case only to find out that someone was just playing a prank. He had used remote control to open and close doors and passages in such a way as to bamboozle onlookers. Maliki therefore decided to try and find out what it was all about by himself later that very night.

Around two in the morning he left his room and went to hide near the shrine. He waited patiently for them to come out, but instead another three men came out from the church. They looked around as if they were criminals trying to make sure that no one had seen them before going to stand by one edge of the slab. With Agnes in his hand he came out and joined them on the slab. One of them tried to protest but Agnes silenced him. The remaining two claimed that they were there just to check on any donations that had been made to the Madonna. They usually stole any gifts and that was their only means of livelihood. He shot the one that gave that explanation for lying, and it was only then that the last one knew that he had no choice but to let the cat out of the bag. He offered to give him a ride down. All he had to do was to pull the Madonna's ear and the other half of the slab slid downwards like an elevator to the depth of about eight feet while another slab slid across to cover them right away. To go back out all he had to do was just to match out since this time around it would be an automatic door. Maliki bound him up after stripping him naked and also gagged him with duct tape across his mouth.

He put on the man's dress over his own and hurried down the flight of stairs that was there. That led him to a burial crypt. There was a side door there and it led up into the church. He checked out three of the crypts that were nearest to him and they contained the embalmed bodies of their last three prelates.

He could not find any other exit and that was a little bit confusing. He kept touching everything that he saw there until he came to the tomb of bishop Opanheimer. Guessing from what the name sounded like, he opened the crypt, but instead of his embalmed body it contained a statue of him. He pulled on the right ear and there it was. Just as with Ali Baba and his "open sesame' command in Ali Baba and the forty thieves, part of the wall on one side slid open. He found himself face to face with a passageway. It was all dark, dank and spooky inside the passageway as he stepped in playing it by the ears. He could hear movements and some noise somewhere far away and he headed there with the aid of his pencil touch.

It was a maze that went from one catacomb to the other and it seemed to be endless. He however got closer to the source of the noise that he had heard. They were voices. They were coming from a brightly lit arena and he stole to the corner by the arena where he hid. There were about fifty men there practicing the martial arts and they all had the same type of dress as he was wearing over his own. Two of them had familiar faces. It then dawned on him. They were two of the men that he had trained with at Dambatta. They were in the class that graduated just as he was coming in. The bigger one was their instructor. He finally made up his mind as to what cause of action to take. He just matched in and faced the instructor.

"Who are you?" The instructor bellowed in surprise. He was huge and he looked intimidating, but he was no match for Maliki.

"My name is Maliki."

"And what are you here for?"

"To join up."

"Where are your guides?"

"There was an emergency and so they had to go back. They told me that they were going to be back in about thirty minute's time."

Just at that moment the other man remembered his face. He had stood out during their graduation. He shouted:

"That's Maliki. I remember him now. That was the man that we were told was a beggar from a village that had been wiped out by some missile."

That made the instructor a little bit more relaxed

"Have you met some of these boys before?" He asked.

""Yes that is Isa." And he pointed at one boy in the second row." He was in the class after me."

"What is your current assignment?"

"I am going in as a suicide bomber in the old city, but I was told that I had to come over here to brush up a little bit more on my tactics."

"Good. You just came in at the right moment. We are just in the middle of the first lesson so go down and join the last row."

Maliki joined the last row as they practiced a couple of kung fu and karate moves. As soon as he got ready for action he brought out Agnes. He was going to take out all of them since they were all trained terrorists, but he planned to keep the instructor alive till the end. He hoped to pry out a few facts from him. As it had been with his most recent actions, he let Agnes make the opening moves. By the time they realized what was happening, most of them were already dead. He dodged from side to side to avoid attackers while squeezing out deadly slugs from Agnes as each bullet successfully brought down one man.

He had come onto them in absolute furry. To him, they had done many things of which not even God Himself could forgive any of them. He was going to attend to them with utmost dispatch, and he was just doing that. He was usually claimed to be a very considerate man and so he was not the type who would like to create widows out of some innocent women that he did not know or had never met. Unfortunately for these men however, they were single, divorced or at least separated, as they were apt to do considering their professions and behaviors. That was enough excuse for him not to be lenient. Most of them were single and free. He felt that they were only as single as tornadoes in which case they were each free to go anywhere they wished and also to cause as much havoc as they wished.

During the melee, some of them out of confusion actually hit each other, and as soon as his bullets were spent he changed over to his martial arts moves. His patented solid club member karate chops had sent many of them to their graves. He would tighten his palm to a solid chopping edge and with that he would slash away at an angle of forty-five degrees at the junction of the neck and the body. That was usually enough to cut off air supply to the lungs, blood supply to the brains and most importantly initiate cerebral denervation. It would break whichever vertebra was there to cut up the spinal cord in order to effect this denervation. Six of them had quickly fallen to these chops before he decided to change over to the use of his legs.

The first person to experience the fury of his legs had gotten an explosive kick to his groins and that sent him reeling on the floor. He was confused and was not sure as to whether to grab his groins or to go for the pains that were radiating to other areas from there, and to make matters worse he was beginning to throw up. He tried to cover his mouth and Maliki assumed that he was afraid that his heart might attempt to escape from there as his stomach also made an attempt at turning inside out. His ghost made its exit while he was still in pains. It was not going to be a happy ghost.

The next man received a devastating pile driver head butt to his mouth. This one more or less chocked in his own teeth. As he came down from this move in a cork-screw spin, his leg took the next victim on the chest and he fell backwards and hit his head on a ledge. That was the end of him. Three more victims went down before he came to the instructor.

Everyone is destined to die. The difference between individuals is when and how each person is destined or ordained by fate to pass on. For this particular matriculant however, he had just been irreversibly initiated into that cult and communion of the dead. He had been long overdue for this definitive act because he had always threaded and hovered precariously along that fine line between the domains of the living and the dead. He was not exactly outstanding in any given field of human endeavor and so neither side was particularly eager to welcome him. He had been of no apparent desiderative significance and so his demise had gone with a total disregard for due process – funeral obsequies did not apply.

This instructor was a martial arts master though not an expert in it. That was obvious from his behavior. He had taken a good look at Maliki and then sidestepped, and shuffled a little bit. He then paused to loosen his muscles around that nearly absent neck before he beckoned at Maliki to bring it on. If bring it on was what he wanted, that was what Maliki gave to him. He flew into the air towards the instructor but he landed squarely on the ground right in front of him. This was quickly followed by another move. Before the man could realize what was the plan he had bent low and swept him off his feet, and before he could hit the floor Maliki was up. The man also sprang up, too stupefied by the fact that he did not see that move coming and that was both disheartening and annoying.

The shuffling resumed, but this time around it was with more earnestness. Maliki stood his grounds and watched while awaiting even the slightest opportunity to present itself. To the credit of the instructor, Maliki was himself surprised when a Flash Gordon punch found its way to his face. That made him feel dizzy just for an instant. That instant was however enough for his assailant to make another move. He landed a vicious sidekick to his chest and that sent Maliki flying to a wall where he fell against the wall. The instructor then made a very big mistake. He stood there, hands akimbo and kept smiling at him in a derisive manner.

It was a mistake that many fighters make, in total disregard to the basic rules of combat – never relent or let off when the advantage is with you. That pause was his unmaking. Maliki came up spinning on his left arm with feet swishing through the air. It was as if a whirlwind was approaching the instructor. He had never witnessed the like of this before and he was going to see more. The entire movement then turned into a blur with speed as it switched from a vertical approach to a horizontal one, and then it suddenly swooshed past from in-between his legs. He received a stinging kick to his testicles as it passed and the pain that came from it was absolutely indescribable.

As he bent down to attend to that excruciating pain, Maliki took him into a headlock while using his feet to immobilize his arms. The instructor immediately realized that his time was up. Suddenly however Maliki eased off a little bit on his neck before asking:

"I am going to ask a few questions and your replies will decide on whether you are going to live or die."

"Please!" That was all that could come out of him.

"Please what?"

"Please let me live."

"Your life is in your own hands."

"How?"

"Your answers will decide on what happens."

"Ok."

"What is your connection with the ADELA?"

"What is the ADELA?"

The only answer he received from Maliki was that he tightened the chokehold just by one more notch and that was enough to make him change his answer.

"I am in charge of sending off the suicide bombers to their respective destinations as well as making sure that they are fit."

"Whom do you account to?"

"I don't know his name but he comes here once in a while to bring our pay."

"I am aware of the fact that you are telling a lie but let that be. When did you last see Nidal?"

He swallowed hard and took a pause before trying to talk. Maliki had expected that reaction. No one that works for that man will not be afraid to mention his name, not to talk of betraying him.

"Who is Nidal?"

Once more without an answer Maliki gave one more squeeze and he did not know when he began to talk.

"I have never seen him in person. He only sends letters as our instructions."

"Where are the letters then?"

"They are in the crypt of Bishop Judas."

"Bishop Judas?"

"Yes there was a bishop with that name and he was worse than the Judas of the bible. For this reason no one ever goes to his crypt and that is why we use it as our documentary office."

"Who built this place?"

"It was built in the middle ages and so we do not know."

"Are you trying to tell me that the remote control that you people use to open the door was put into place in the middle Ages?"

"No. That was the renovation that came from Nidal and his cronies."

"Where can I find them?"

"I am not too sure of that but they were claimed to always come from the tiny island of Intipuchu."

Maliki had gotten all the information he felt were available and so he tightened the hold. Air was soon cut off from the instructor's lungs as he passed on. He danced a little bit of that jitterbug before taking off to join the other souls who had just died as well as many who had been buried in these crypts and catacombs.

He eventually located that crypt that belonged to Bishop Judas and from there he salvaged their files. The most recent letter was the one that informed them that Nidal had just commissioned a submarine that was based in the island of Intipuchu. Its name was the Amala. He did not specify what it was going to be used for neither did he make any effort to describe it. Maliki however came to the conclusion that he was probably planning to use it to launch some cruise missiles and maybe he had nuclear warheads and dirty bombs that he might be hiding under the sea.

When he emerged from the crypt he was already planning his next move. As soon as he got back to the hotel he started to make arrangements for a trip to that island. He rented a small speedboat for the two-hour journey through very rough seas; The Island was actually exactly fifty miles away from Emor. He was off to the island that very morning.

Intipuchu Island was easy to approach and it had a natural calm cove on its eastern shore and that was where he docked. He moored in one of the piers there before taking off to explore the place. The Island was about one quarter of a mile in diameter, almost round and as flat as a plateau. It was mainly rocky with little patches of sand and grassy areas. Beyond these, it could be taken as a barren Island. It was claimed that there used to be some aboriginal natives there who used the Island as a sacrificial platform for their sea deities in ancient times. There seemed to be no imminent danger or even feelings of it as he went through the entire Island. Since he did not see anything, he decided to take a second tour while believing that the dead instructor had probably planted that document in his files to lure intruders to the Island.

The entire Island seemed to have been formed from denuded igneous rock. With time the adverse denudatory effects of waves, winds, rain and floods had broken the rocks into various sizes from boulders through pebbles to sandy grit. This was how those patchy sandy outcrops came to be. A tract of sandy beaches, which came as deposits from the deep seas by the fierce tides and waves, ringed the entire Island.

It was a mere coincidence for him to have noticed a slight abnormality in the northern shore. The water looked rather too deep blue and so he decided to check it out. When he suited up in his diving gear and went down, it was only to discover that the shore there was a sheer underwater cliff. The wall presented a near ninety-degree perpendicularity. It seemed to be very deep there and so he came back up to get ready to go further down, moreover he had the feeling that something was far below there. It could be part of a reef, which was very common there, or it could be a sunken vehicle. He however felt that it must be the submarine that he came to look for.

Luckily he was ready for very deep sea diving and he got ready for that. He went back and dived down there and it was only to come across a submarine that was more than a hundred yards long. It was a very huge one and how one person could have acquired this puzzled him. As he quietly swam around it, he came across the inscription – "ASYP" – and he immediately translated this to mean "Adela Shipping Yards Plc." He now remembered how it happened. Nidal had once set up that ship scrapping company and it was their duty to help the maritime community tear down their ships to salvage any usable parts. This must be how he outfitted this submarine. He must have outfitted it rather than scrap it and this was going to be his naval base. This is how the Island came to be uninhabited and yet was his base. He circled it a few times and he found out that it was a nuclear powered submarine. His immediate thought was to wait for it to surface one of these days to give him the opportunity to board, but then he could as well take out the hatch and let water rush in to drown whoever was in it.

He finally settled on blowing up the hatch to force them out. Though he did not use his explosives at Emor for respect of the church above it, this was the time for it. He attached one to either side of the hatch and swam up before detonating them. He watched the explosion produce a high water spout as well as a spiraling funnel of water as it rushed in through the opening created by the explosion. As he had expected, they tried to surface the submarine but it was too late and it sank faster than it rose.

Many people tried to swim out. They were of course Nidal's men and so he was not going to take pity on them. This also reminded him that three cargo ships and one frigate had actually vanished into thin air not too far from this area in the not too distant past. When one of the ships was salvaged from the depths all its crew were gone together with the gold bullion that it was transporting to the vaults of the central bank of one of the newly independent oil rich countries. As for the frigate, apart from the ships mates, all her cruise missiles were also gone. It had remained a deep-sea mystery but this submarine was the answer.

The submarine had finally settled for the sea bed as the men tried to swim out. Maliki, with the aid of Agnes cut them down as soon as they surfaced. None of them could make it to the shore till his bullets had gotten finished. He therefore braced up and got ready to attack as soon as anyone swam to the shore. He had that big advantage of their having been exhausted by the time they got out.

The first marina to swim out was an experienced and old hand. As he swam out looking tired and exhausted Maliki knew that he was going to have an easy victim; but that old flute still had some tones left in it! The old man had no time to ask questions. As soon as he set eyes on Maliki he knew that he had come face to face with the source of their misfortune and calamity. He immediately went into a dizzying series of cartwheel summersaults that brought him within two feet of Maliki. Then with an enviable promptitude and amazing rapidity he let out a flurry of karate kicks. They were very fast and accurate but they now lacked reasonable momentum. The swimming and near drowning experience had left him much weakened. Maliki then went up into the air in a gravity-defying maneuver that let him come down from the top. With a powerful kick that seemed to defy all possible kinetic calculations he let the sailor have it to his neck. He immediately became history.

The next two to swim ashore had witnessed the attack and so they each took the easier egress. That did not worry Maliki since the only way out of the Island was by boat and the keys were in his pocket. They soon realized the futility of any efforts to run away and so they doubled back and decided to make a stand. Unfortunately, the expressions on their faces told the entire story. It was that type of expression that could only be a pure distillate of nascent realization – the realization that they were face to face with death.

The impetus with which Maliki rammed his head into the mid torso area of the closest sailor left no lingering thoughts of what was going to happen. The second man therefore took off in a flat out sprint into the wide-open Island. He was not yet ready to die. The topography of the Island was not exactly encouraging and there seemed to be no easy way out. The driving force that led to this attempt did not take time to fizzle out. To remain alive was no longer a viable option and so once more he doubled back. This was after he cleared a knoll only to find out that it was just a wide expanse of ocean over there ahead of him. This was why he had come back once more, and it was with more determination. However, it was only one single swoop from Maliki that sent his soul to the nether world. It was a vilifying crab claw strike. He was dead long before Maliki could get his fingers to his chest with the full intent of ripping out his soul.

The next two men that swam out were equally unlucky. Having just managed to extricate themselves from that watery abyss, none of them was in the mood for any fight. There was no inclination at all from any of them towards any resistance whatsoever. All they did was to scamper. There was no need to loiter around this death-infested Island and they could try anything to remain alive, including defection, if that was possible. One of them was more forthcoming. He came closer to Maliki and pled for mercy. Maliki had no time to mess around with any evil men and so he simply went back to his boat and retrieved a few more magazines. With Agnes now once more ready for action he took mercy on the poor man and shot him point blank. He hunted down all the other men and helped each go under. As he was just about to leave, he noticed a slight movement from the corner of his eye. It was a lady getting up from the sands.

She had witnessed everything that took place and she was also too exhausted to even plead for mercy. As soon as he turned towards her, that sent shivers through her together with a few muffled and embarrassing anno-rectal effusions. She was sure that this man must be an evil mutant of the devil. He was a complete killing machine and he was merciless. To her, he had materialized in that Island in the full similitude to that grim reaper. As for the killing, she was right, but when it came to his being evil, that was where she got it wrong several times over. He was there only to eliminate the evil ones and unfortunately she was one of them. She eventually found her voice and so she tried to trade her life for some information as to what was going on in the submarine.

Maliki therefore showed her that he was a gentleman, and that he was when one comes to think of it. He flashed a smile at her, pretending to be very interested in her. It was one of those suggestive smiles. It should be remembered at this juncture that he was only pretending. This is still the same man who is very allergic to members of the opposite sex. He was of the opinion that whenever they are introduced or injected into any equation, something was bound to go wrong. This was because they were always a source of distraction for the men, especially when they are as beautiful as this blue-eyed nymph that was there in front of him. He was not going to take any chances with her, but he had to go along with her all the same.

"What information do you think that I will be interested in my dear?" That was how he put it.

"About what we have been doing in the submarine."

"What makes you think that I will be interested in that?"

"From how you have been taking out my colleagues, my guess is that you have been after us for some time now.

Furthermore it is obvious that it was you who blew open the hatch to the submarine."

"Your colleagues?"

"Yes. My name is Natasha, and they all work under me."

"I am happy to meet you, but what was your business in that submarine?"

"Please promise not to kill me and I will tell you the whole story."

"I promise."

"But who are you to start with?"

"I am a United Nations agent, and my name is Maliki."

"I have never heard of you."

"I am just a low level operative."

"We are scientists performing some experiments."

"I don't think that you have to beat about the bush as to what you actually do."

"How?"

"What's your connection to Nidal?"

"How did you find out about that?"

"The inscription on the submarine."

"Ok. It belongs to him."

"And where is he right now?"

"He could be in any of his numerous bases."

"What is your connection with all those ships that have been missing in recent times?"

"We take out some of them for the money and others for arms and equipments."

"Like the gold bullion in the 'Pacific Interlocutor'?"

"Yes."

"What of the frigate that got missing last month?"

"That was just for the guided missiles that it was carrying."

"I guessed so, but what do you plan to do with them?"

"Actually all we wanted was the guidance system so that we could study it."

"Why not just that then? You took the entire missile systems as well."

"That was just to make sure that investigators are thrown off the scent."

"What is the truth then?"

"Nidal wants us to study those guidance systems so that we could use them to disarm military satellites. After that he would deploy his own satellites and with the information from these ones we would have a foolproof system. It would therefore be possible for him to change the commands to any weapons that are controlled via satellites and send them to his own destinations. In short one country could launch a missile to hit an opponent and he would be able to turn it around so that it could come back home. To put it in another way, you could launch a nuclear headed missile and he would get it to make a U turn and come back to hit you instead."

"Of what use could that prank be to him?"

"He plans to get all the nuclear powers to launch their

missiles and destroy each other rather than use them to inconvenience others. To him, it was an easy way of achieving nuclear disarmament. Anyone who witnesses the destruction this will cause will think twice before venturing into making any such weapon."

"That sounds convincing but there are other ways of achieving that."

"Like what other ways?"

"Through negotiations for instance."

"While that is going on, as it has been doing for quite some time now, has it occurred to you that more people are going into that?"

"You might be right about that, but taking the laws into your own hands does not seem to be the right move."

"Anyway he also planned to establish his own space station. From there he would take out anyone that did not agree with him."

"Now you are talking. Don't you per chance think that the entire thing seems to boarder on madness?"

"I agree with you completely when it comes to that. The fact is that one should not forget that there is only a very thin line between madness and sanity and each encroaches into the domains of the other."

"I can see that you are quite educated."

"Why do you say so?"

"Going by your line of reasoning you could be a philosopher."

"Actually I hold four PhDs. My field of expertise includes aeronautic engineering, biology, philosophy and business administration."

"How I wish that you had channeled your talents into more positively fruitful pursuits."

"But that's what I am into."

"You see the mind is free to float through and flirt with all possibilities, but when it comes to the body, it is a different story. The body has to remain within the strict confines of human laws. You have gone far beyond the confines of these laws simply by being a terrorist and I believe that for that reason, it is about time for you to die."

"But what of that your promise to let me live?"

"I was only lying."

With that he let Agnes drill a neat hole through the center of her forehead. She died right away.

After this he called the secretary of state at home and told him where they should go to recover the submarine. That would also help them know what had happened to all those missing ships. After that he took his boat and sailed back to the mainland before taking off to continue with his quest – to hunt down Nidal.

From what she had told him, Nidal could be in any of his hideouts. However he favored Sirap. That was where most of the letters he had come across came from. He was known to frequent the central museum of arts and culture there. Most of those letters actually came from a post office that was very close to the museum.

It was barely a day after this incidence before he was once more off. He took another trans-oceanic flight to Sirap.

From Sirap to Ogba Caverns

As soon as Maliki landed at the Sirap international airport, he went straight to check into a nearby hotel – *"La Grande Femme"*. He checked into a penthouse suite on the twenty first floor. From up there he could see most of the land locked city, which was the capital of Basque. Just like Emor, this was a very old city if not much older. It was famed for having one of the most elaborate sewage systems on earth.

Natasha had hinted that the hotel was a favorite rendezvous for members of the ADELA. By the time he had spent three days there he was still not on to any luck. There was no news of the organization neither had he seen anything unusual. Out of boredom he decided to go down for a drink - quite out of character for Maliki. He however went down as a different man. He went down in a three piece Italian suite while disguised as a bearded old sailor. A lush mustache and a fairly long goatee disguised his face. He remained unrecognized by anyone who knew him before, either as Ike or as Maliki.

After a few rounds of drinks he went over to the gentleman's club section of the longue. This "red district" club occupied most of the basement. He had figured that it was there that most of the shady characters might congregate and he was right. It was a fairly exclusive strip tease club and the girls there came in various imaginable as well as unimaginable shapes and sizes. This was done on purpose. It would carter for every imaginable taste. They ranged from the skinny to the amorphous, as well as from the very tall to near dwarfs and cretins. It was a matter of choice. He sank into a comfortable sofa by one dimly lit corner and from there he surveyed the entire place. Many of the men there looked like irresponsible hoodlums but he did not fail to notice that they all seemed to know each other. Some of the girls were young enough to be teenagers, and he was also sure that one of the women must be in her seventies.

These ladies would dance and strip on the stage and then come down to mingle with the men. They were each barely clad in anything at all. This was a very good strategy because the men doled out wads of money and literarily emptied their pockets. His intuition or rather premonition was telling him that he was up to something big, but he could not yet seem to lay his hands on it. He was therefore very ready for any unexpected eventualities. Three of the girls passed by his table and then suddenly stopped. Each of them seemed to be interested in him. He was actually still all that any girl with a head over her shoulders would wish for – tall, particularly handsome even in his disguise, gentlemanly, athletically built with rather huge biceps whose profiles could be seen through his sleeves and he had a soothingly nice voice. All that came from him was a 'hai' to none of them in particular. They all landed on his laps without warning and at the same time. He found that extremely uncomfortable but he just had to go along with them. He looked on as they struggled for who would get the best of him. It eventually led to a little fight.

One of them had thrown a bottle at the other but she missed her target. The bottle hit a lonely hoodlum and he did what should be expected of his type. In short within minutes it had turned into a free for all fight. Bottles flew around as missiles and many were simply hoisted up and slammed on the floor. Tables were overturned as punches flew in every given direction with the target of each punch being whoever was closest to the fist. The only thing that did not happen was for one to hit himself. Once in a while he would dunk from a flying missile, be it bottle or human.

He remained in the safety of that corner watching what was going on and enjoying the fight. At length one of the ladies ran over and dragged him out with the explanation that she was taking him to safety. He followed her as she took him down one flight of stairs into a tight portion of the basement. It was within one tight nook under the stairs that she finally gave him a hint of what was her true intention. She suddenly ripped off her brazier as well as her bikini underwear. Maliki had been cornered and for once he was unsure of himself. He blushed and then fell on his knees to beg her to postpone the act. He said that it was not that he was not interested but that he would prefer a more comfortable and safer place. She probably thought that he was telling the truth and so she unlatched the door that was very near there.

Maliki suddenly found himself within a lofty tunnel as wide as a dual carriageway. There was however a slowly moving slushy and foul smelling effluent flowing at the center of the tunnel. It was the famed Sirap central underground sewage system. The foul smell only had a hint of the sewage, which it was. The entire tunnel was well lighted and ventilated in most areas, and once in a while they will come across a locked up side room. This lady, Ingrid, claimed that this was the sewage system and that she was very familiar with every inch of it. According to her, those side rooms were used in those days to store chemicals used in the sewage treatment. In the more modern times they have a central treatment facility and so most of the rooms were now defunct. She did not have enough money to pay for rent in this costly city and so she must have taken over one of the rooms. Maliki remembered that the ADELA had something to do with the hotel and this might be it.

On his prompting she had explained that there were smaller tunnels here and there but that they all discharged into this central one. Those rooms that seemed to be built on a higher level than the rest were actually being used by drug dealers and at times the users too. The water level always rose with the rains, but they usually went down again within minutes and that was why the place came to look so neat. The floodwaters always washed the place very clean. When he asked whether there were other buildings connected to the tunnel like the hotel the answer was an emphatic no. The usual entrances were through the utility manholes which were everywhere along the roads. Most of the criminals and the other unofficial occupants and users of the system went in through these manholes except for the group that operated from the hotel. She had informed him that this was a very mysterious and secretive group and that most of the men in the gentleman's club were from that group.

On further enquiry he found out that she was a very close confidant and look out for the leader of the group who was the albino that was in the club. Maliki knew that he had to do what he had to do about this. He was sure that these were the men that he was after. He was going to take out all of them, but he was going to save the albino for the last. This might give him the opportunity to find out more about Nidal from him. His name was Niki. She eventually steered him into one of the rooms and that was her apartment. He got her to dress up and then explained to her that she should escape through one of the manholes back to the hotel. Something bad was about to happen and he did not want her to be involved or to be injured till they meet again later the following evening. She was used to men of the underworld and such a request was not unusual to her and so she took off right away. She knew that there were going to be a few killings and she also knew that the only way to remain safe was to keep quiet. To him she was only guilty by association and knew next to nothing about what was going on. He was going to let her live.

After she left, he ran back to one of the rooms that they had passed on their way. This was the one that she claimed that Niki was fond of going into, but that he had never allowed her to see what was there. It was a bare room with nothing in it but a small safe in one corner. He had picked the lock to gain entrance into it. When he succeeded in opening the safe it was exactly as he had expected. There were only letters in it. There was however a small square box there that was used to weigh the letters down. When he opened it, he was surprised to find out that it was full of diamonds, and underneath the letters was a small accounting ledger. The ledger had the names of all those bases that he had taken out, how much each made or used, allocations to each and what the allocations were for. There were also entries from their different bank accounts. They were involved in a lot of cyberspace activities and that was what the last document there was all about.

It indicated that their cyberspace activities were being run from the Ogba caverns somewhere in Africa. It was there that they had the most complete set of professionals in all areas of Endeavour Nidal paid a lot of money for these people to come over to work for him there. He often invited them with offers that none of them could ever resist. One professor of nuclear physics for instance that used to be on a salary of two hundred thousand dollars in a research institute in his country was invited over there at a salary of twelve million dollars per annum, tax paid. The specialty of this place was however in the cyberspace front. Their main duty was to send viruses to other computers especially military computers and those that controlled satellites. They also managed to link up to bank computers and databases from there. It was in this way that they were able to transfer money from other people's accounts into their own. They concentrated on those accounts that were such that their owners will never report any losses. Drug dealers were topmost in their list as well as corrupt public officials and heads of states. It was therefore the main brain to the entire set up and it was therefore imperative that Nidal had to spend most of his time around there. Maliki now sensed that his quest was nearing its end.

His most revealing discovery was that Niki was the second in command to Nidal. It was from there that they planned to control all military satellites, redirect launched missiles as well as debrief other satellites. He waited by one side for Niki and his men to come for the night. They would usually wait till the nightclub closed around two in the morning before going down for a meeting. Maliki closed the door behind him and waited in one corner of the room.

Three of his men were the first to come into the room. It was a very wise arrangement. If there was going to be any trouble it would start with those men and that advance party would warn him in time. They did not however see him from where he was hiding. Niki always wanted to remain anonymous and never liked to attract attention to himself. He therefore came into the room and closed the door behind him just at the same moment as Maliki appeared from where he was hiding. They were all surprised and puzzled at his being there, but it was very unfortunate that they were each pathetically ignorant of what was about to take place there or happen to them.

He did not give them enough time to recover from their surprises before he took a recumbent position from where he made a peculiar move, which sort of triangulated them in respect to his position. This apparent triangulation sort of brought one of them directly in front of him and he went down without any warning to a Polish hammer blow to his chest, without any of them knowing what the attack was all about. Another two approached him from either side with the hope of a kill. They were all used to instantaneous fights, especially those free for all types that were typical of drinking bars, and so they were ready and eager to fight. What they did not however expect was what happened to them next. They came diagonally from either side when he suddenly leapt some three feet from the floor and then kicked sideways as they approached. Each instep connected perfectly to its target between the legs. They each doubled up with pain as he elevated himself once more, in a manner that was defiant of all the laws of gravity. Each man immediately received a present. It was a well-executed Kung Fu kick to the nape of the neck. They each fell down and died with broken vertebrae. With that he escaped through the door into the tunnel. They followed suit together with some newcomers. They were of the opinion that he was on the run, but they were wrong. He just wanted more room to maneuver and deal with them.

He was not at all disappointed as a group of six more men joined in the fight right away. Niki remained behind like a field marshal to assess the situation. He still carried his head quite high with pride irrespective of all his ignoble acts, ways and ignominious activities. As they negotiated that very gentle declivity of the tunnel, Maliki made his move. They were still about halfway between the side door from which they had emerged and the room and so there was not going to be anywhere to hide from him. Three of them tried to go for their guns but it was a mistake. They only attracted his attention and Agnes materialized out of nowhere and cut them down before any of them could complete his draw. That was enough to make the rest not to think of that at all. She spat out a few more slugs almost at random and five of them were already down. He dived towards the other group while sprinting towards them with Agnes pointed in their general direction. It was a zig- zagging dive and Agnes was spitting out hot lead all the while as his decumbency helped to make him present a hard target for anyone who could be aiming from a hidden area. The rest fell to her hot leads.

The fairly humid atmosphere of this underground territory, the dankness of the entire alleyways, and the fairly thin oxygen level had combined to take its toll on them. The alcohol that they had taken worsened this. More had come in, but they were all panting despite the fact that the fight was still in its infancy. He hit the first man that he approached so hard that his skin immediately remembered that it was a semi permeable membrane. Water and various other salts began to move from their various areas of high concentrations in the body to the skin as sweat. It was that type of sweat that is hard to explain away, but it came in abundance.

It took an adjectival double blow to send him to blazes. It started off with a crab claw punch, which gored his eyes, while the even more deadly and more devastating show stopper kick ended it all. The lethality of this unholy alliance of karate moves could only best be left to the imagination. It would however be worthwhile to point out that his soul left his body without being very sure of how it was released. Even his body went stiff without remembering to dance its farewell jitterbug dance – its rigor mortis.

Finally he was face to face with Niki. Neither of these two fighters was able to hide his true feelings when they set eyes on each other. There was that intrinsic mutually assured distrust between them. It was a distrust that was so intense that it immediately and instantly fanned up those latent ambers of intractable and total hatred from deep down within each. The albino had no way of trusting anyone who had managed to intrude and infiltrate his secrete underground base, and he had the right to feel so. Maliki on his own part could never come to terms with the fact that a man who had been rumored to be particularly austere with words should not at least resort to hiding his feelings towards others. To him it amounted to an irrepressible disregard for others. Besides that, he was one of the arms of the devil that he was after. That was the basis for that mutual distrust and hatred of each other.

Maliki suddenly sprang up and with a triple somersault he set himself on Niki who had changed to causing him, probably in an attempt to psych him out. Niki had no gun with him otherwise he would have shot Maliki, but despite the fact that he stood there with the stance of a martial arts expert, his uncontrollable vociferous ribaldry would be a disgrace even to the very scum of the society. It was a tirade of diverse acrimonious nonsense but Maliki kept his cool and he still had his plans for this man who he now considered to be mere excrement. Before he got too close, hoping that Niki was only bluffing, he received a solid punch full to his face. He did not see that coming.

Niki was fast. He was dazed for just the fraction of a second by that punch but that was enough time for this his worthy assailant to make his next move. He received a karate chop to his clavicle and that was enough to send him to his knees. Had Maliki finally met his match? No way!

He simply grabbed the man's testicles and squeezed as hard as he could. Maliki knew how to fight dirty. Niki let out a very loud shout of agony as Maliki hoisted him up with that hold and slammed him hard to the floor. The albino was now completely red in color. Maliki did not waste any time before putting him into a double anaconda headlock. Niki immediately realized that death would be on its way if he did not do anything about it. Through his gasping breath therefore he asked to be pitied. Maliki released the hold only a very small fraction before asking him about where he could find Nidal. Niki would not answer but he reminded him that he could always give a little more squeeze. He was also just one more squeeze away from death. He now realized that he was going to die if he did not play along, but he may have some chances to live if he did, no matter how slim.

It was only then that Niki told him that Nidal was at the Ogba caverns somewhere in Africa. He was going to be there for at least the next three weeks. Now that Maliki had got what he wanted, he completed the squeeze and waited till he heard the vertebrae break. He abandoned the body there to rest with his pals and then found his way back to the hotel.

The very first thing that Maliki did in the morning was to get his things ready in a hurry and leave in a charter flight for the Ogba caverns. This was somewhere in the central part of Africa and he had a fairly good idea of where it was. He had heard of it a long time ago.

While in the plane to Africa, Maliki tried to recall all that he could remember about the Ogba Caverns. It was claimed to be a natural system of caves and passages, some of them small and others very big. The system originated from a small volcanic hill. Many small streams traverse the caverns and in ancient times it was the domain of a dreaded oracle. It was however discovered, much later in history, that the idea of an oracle there was a trick. A group of unscrupulous entrepreneurs had only used the idea to pry into the beliefs of the people and extract as much money from them as possible. Its main entrance was through a small opening by the hill. A massive oracle shrine was built over this entrance. It was the most dreaded oracle and arbiter in the land. It went on for well over five miles to come out in a smaller shrine by a riverbank. This was the dreaded shrine of the mermaids. These businessmen had transformed their empire into a close-knit secret cult to run the racket.

They freely terrorized people in the immediate neighborhoods of the hill and always managed to get them to pay homage to the oracle of the hill. They had to pay for the continued protection of their people by the oracle. Most importantly however was the fact that this oracle had become very famous and was consulted by clients from far and wide. It had become a respected arbiter in cases of serious disputes. The aggrieved parties would come to the shrine at the entrance of the system to present their grievances to the high priest to the oracle. This incidentally was the chief executive officer of the enterprise. In minor cases the guilty party would pay a fine to the oracle as well as pay the consultation fee for either side.

In more serious cases however the punishment is usually death. This was very common with murder as well as with land disputes amongst others. In such cases each side would be asked to match into the cave at ten minutes intervals. Only the innocent would be able to return. Officially the oracle would dispose of the guilty party and return the innocent. In reality the "guilty" were actually led through the system to it's other exit by the river. This was the shrine of the mermaids. This was during the slave trade era and they were actually sold into slavery from there straight to the traders in their boats. The slaves were transported to stations and outposts from where they were taken overseas never to be seen again. It was not until one of the slaves came back after over thirty years overseas that he told his story and the whole scheme ended with members of the cult running away.

The caverns were therefore sealed off, but they were

opened up many years later as a source of income. It had become a source of tourist attraction and many adventurists would go through the system. Nidal had bought a lot of land here above the hill and he had built an estate there. He had erected a fortress in the middle of the estate and that was where he lived. As usual it was ingeniously designed. The fortress was a three-story building and he lived on the third floor. One of his wardrobes had a secret button behind his line of clothes and this was the control for his private elevator. This elevator ran through the middle of the wall as a pillar down into one of the caverns in the cave. From this cavern he had sealed off three others together with it. From the outside, which is from within the cavern system, it would just be the usual stonewall that marked the end of many blind alleys there. These four caverns served as the head quarters of the ADELA.

Most of this information was what he had extracted from Niki before he left to join his ancestors. According to him, not more than a handful, probably less than three, of people had ever been inside the place. The plane finally landed in the international airport in Jalingo, which was the country in which the caves were situated. From the airport he rented a car and made straight for the estate. He approached the Ogba hills very cautiously while taking note of everything around. He was sure of the fact that Nidal was going to be extra careful and on the watch out since he must have gotten the news of the recent loss of some of his bases. By the time that he got to the fortress he realized that it was even more imposing that as he had expected. The houses in the estate were few and each was quite far apart from the other. Some were more than a hundred yards away from each other. He could see a few of the residents going home or just coming out and he knew that this part of the estate was there just as a buffer zone for his fortress. The fortress was exactly in the mathematical and geometrical middle of the estate.

The fortress had an eight feet high wall as its fence and there was just one small entrance to the place. It was however a sprawling compound inside. The big three-story building was there just as he had been told. Every building in the estate came with a large satellite dish and the roads were very well paved. At the entrance to the estate was a sign that read *"paradise estates."* That was exactly what Niki had told him. Maliki decided that it would be better to enter the place at night and it was already dusk so he drove back into town before returning. His car was the make and color that was most common in the place and for this he did not stand out. It was just one of those cars.

He came back and waited from not too far away until he saw a car about to drive into the fortress. He let the car drive in before he came to the gateman. When the gateman wanted to know whom he was as well as for his identification, he produced the most easily read of all his documents. That was Agnes! The man immediately recognized the identification and so opened the gate wide enough for him to come in. Agnes had her silencer on, and so just as the man finished closing back the gate he was shot. This was necessary to avoid the chances of anyone raising an alarm. He dragged the body into the booth and then continued to the back of the building as he had seen the other car do.

There were a few cars parked there and so he eased his own in-between two others and then headed for the door. Though the main door was in front of the house, an ornate door, it seemed that this smaller door at the back was his main door. The front door was for visitors while the back one was for the inhabitants of the building and they were just Nidal and his guards. There did not seem to be any key or knob for the door and so he believed that it must be an automatic door, but nothing happened as he got there. When however he tried to rap on it the door swung open. That was how that door was made. Rather than sensing an approaching user, it would respond only to the touch of a finger.

It let him into a brightly lit room or rather foyer from its size. The foyer was not furnished. It had just one massive desk right there at the entrance and an equally massive beast sat on it. This reminded him of his escapades with the drug dealers each of which had a few of this breed of humanoids. He knew the implications of seeing that brute there and the brute on his part knew the implications of seeing an intruder there. They were each aware of the fact that there was going to be a fight. When he stood up, he was as much as eight feet tall, and he was massive in every aspect of him. If not that he was Maliki, he would have tried to find his way back out right away. This man mountain was something like regularly irregular. For instance, his biceps looked normal on his left arm but on the right they were disproportionately large. While one of his eyes was as much as closed the other was so large that it made him look like one of those one eyed Cyclops. His head was massive and what could have been a massive blow had left a large swelling at the center of his forehead, just below his fontanel. This made him look like a human hybrid of the unicorn. His legs were as large and as solid as oak trunks and Maliki knew that he was going to be in for a tough one. He must have to start with something to weaken him and it had to be fast too.

He quickly flashed out Agnes and in no time at all a bullet had found its way into that big eye. The brute simply wiped out the blood that began to issue from there and stood his ground. It was just as if nothing had happened to him. Luck was on the side of Maliki. The brute did not see how he could winch or cry out for pain especially when it was from that diminutive thing in front of him. He was wrong. The next bullet ricocheted off his horn and that was a new experience for Maliki. The next two bullets went for his chest just over his heart but they were of no use. He was wearing bulletproof vests. Maliki was beginning to get impatient as well as worried. It was then that the brute decided to make his own move. He sent a punch towards Maliki but he was able to dodge the massive fist as it approached him. A second one however landed on his forehead. It felt as if a pile driver had just rammed him. He fell down in a daze.

Just after that punch he saw a massive oak trunk in the air coming down towards him again. The prospects of his demise were the only thing that gave Maliki courage. He rolled to one side to avoid the leg while at the same time squeezing out three more bullets in quick succession into his scrotum. That hurt! He did not bellow or cry out as he had expected and that gave him the idea that the brute could have been castrated and he also must have had his tongue cut off. That must be why he had not uttered a single word so far. All he did was to bring down one massive palm to hold on to his scrotum or whatever was there.

By now Maliki had realized that he had weakened the brute enough, moreover one of his hands had now been given a new assignment to keep it out of the fight. He therefore went into full action. He suddenly catapulted himself with a flip out of the way. He found himself about five feet away from the man and it was from there that he executed a flying kung fu kick. It was to the man's neck, but it was a useless move since the man was essentially without a neck. His big head had simply merged into his torso. He then resorted to the topsy-turvy fore finger drill and the other eye was gone too. Now that he was blind, though he still did not as much as give out a mere grunt; Maliki was able to circumnavigate around him with ease and unnoticed. The man had, legally speaking, violated his writ of mandamus. He did not let him pass by without challenge, and so he was going to pay dearly for that. He tried to grope hopelessly in the air and it was only then that Maliki tried what he thought would be best for the man. He did not like to see people suffer for too long. That was his soft side.

He let Agnes send a bullet at point blank range into the position of the nape of his neck. The bullet brushed by the occipital condyle into the brain and he immediately knelt down before falling finally to the ground. Unfortunately for most of the occupants of this fortress, and fortunately for Maliki, each room was fully sound proofed. No one could hear what was going on in the next room. He quickly went through the entire ground floor taking out all the five men that he came across. They included a cook and a butler who were busy getting the night's meals ready.

The last person he came across on this floor was a fairly obese fellow. He was tall but more of a fool than any other thing. He had briefly seen Maliki take out his mate with the aid of Agnes, but certain pretentious sentimentalisms on his part had gotten him to believe that he was going to be left alive. It was a very mendacious assumption and that made him drop his guard. He must be one of those peripatetic ignoramuses that have acquired this obnoxious predisposition towards the belief that they were well trained and huge as well as strong, and so would be able to tackle anyone anywhere. He felt that his size was a great asset and that the intruder was going to be afraid of him. He was very wrong! It took just a single intractable jugular snap kick to help him over to that abode of nothingness. His soul departed with a subdued though malodorous afflatus from his rear end. It was the type that would be expected from and typical of a constipated carrion eater.

The second floor looked like an area used as offices except that it had one massive sitting room. This room had a massive wall-to-wall liquid crystal high definition television screen. That must be where he entertained his guests if he ever had any. Each of the rooms was like a study with a small library. There were ten of them but only two had beds in them to show that they were bedrooms, probably for some of his guards or guests. In short the entire second floor was empty. The dining area had a table with plates on them and evidence that someone had just had a meal there.

He took the stairwell up to the third floor and there he met the same reception as he did when he came in from outside. It looked as if this was the twin brother to the brute that he had tangled with earlier on. The only difference was that this second one had two normal eyes and also he had no horn. He was however slightly bigger than the first one, but rather that to sit on the table like that first one, he was standing hands akimbo in a defiant manner right in front of the room. His face was a mere evil grimace and he looked as if he had been waiting for him to come up. Of course he was. There were the screens to a close circuit system on the table and from there one could see most of the rooms. He probably only saw him in the second floor otherwise he would have been more belligerent. It suddenly dawned on him as to why he was not seen on the first floor. His fellow brute took care of the entrance and he was so efficient that the area was chosen as the blind spot for the system. What a stupid mistake!

Maliki knew that he did not have to waste time since he was not sure of how many of these things that he was going to face. He therefore consulted Agnes who immediately did her part. She sent four bullets flying towards the brute without any warning. Two hit each eye, the third hit his heart and the fourth went straight into his head at the center of his fore head. As Maliki had expected, the bullet meant for his heart only got lodged within his vest, which was bullet proof. That did not deter him as this one gave out a grunt. He therefore sent a fifth bullet into his Adams apple. As the brute tried to open his mouth to say something, he sent a sixth one into it. This took an upward trajectory and it was the one that finally took care of the man. The bullet found it's way through his upper palate and from there into his brains and he was gone. Just like his brother, his knees first buckled and he came down on them as if about to pray before falling forwards face down without any more sounds. It was much later that he found out that he was right about them. They were eunuchs with their tongues cut off. They were bred by Nidal and he sold some of them off to those Mafia dons. What a wicked business! They were not in a position to leak out any secrets.

There was no one in any of the rooms on that floor till he hit the master bedroom. It was a very plush bedroom. There was a king sized bed there with a bedside dressing table. There was a reading desk in front of a window that faced the hills. The bed sheets were slightly wrinkled and the mattress felt warm to the touch, which meant that Nidal was there not too long ago. His next assignment was to locate the button in the wardrobe. The wardrobe was full of shoes, shirts, pants and jackets as well as a few caftans. The second wardrobe was exactly the same as the first but slightly wider and he knew that it must be the one he was looking for especially when considering the fact that it was very close to the pillar. There was however nothing to indicate how to gain entrance into this one. He tried all possible alternatives and there was no hope of getting into it. He tried to consider one funny option – just wait there and he would be back up through there one of these days. One thing however discouraged him from trying out this option. It was possible that this foxy character might have another escape route. He therefore kept trying. If they used a remote control at the shrine of the Madonna then anything was possible with this man.

Just as he guessed, there was a remote control in one of the dressing table drawers – maybe just a duplicate. He tried it out but nothing happened. As he sat down by the wall near the wardrobe in annoyance the door to the wardrobe sprang open. It was then that he realized that the tiny light switch on the floor by the wall was actually the switch to the wardrobe. The second part was to locate the switch to the elevator. Inside it was just like the first, but there was no switch anywhere there and the remote control would not do anything. After he stepped out he tried to close the wardrobe with the switch. As the door was closing he realized that there was a faint swooshing sound coming from inside it. That was the trick. Switch on once and the door opens. Try the second time and it closes while something else opens inside. He gave about a minute and then tried it again. The door opened, then he tried it the second time while stepping into it. Eureka! The entire wardrobe was the elevator. It simply swooshed down to a similar room in the cave.

He carefully stepped out into the room and went around it carefully. He finally tried the door on the left and it led into a computer room. There were just two desktops there and so he came out and tried the next door. It led into another computer room and a man was there clicking away on a keyboard. Whoever it was had to be Nidal, but he did not quite look like what he had expected. This man was nothing to write home about.

He was a very diminutive looking man, simple looking and completely unimpressive. He was however sly looking, complete with shifty eyes. He did not even seem surprised at seeing him. He was obviously well educated and more importantly well mannered. He was also attributed with various powers of hypnotism and magic.

He wore a simple pair of pants and short-sleeved shirt of broadloom brocade. Everything about him, especially his manner of speaking, pointed to his indisputable powers of erudition while his equanimity was unsurpassed. He had however approached the end of all his evil machinations as would soon be seen. The Pandora's box had long been opened and it was about to unleash untold misfortune on him. Most of his men were already gone.

He simply looked up and smiled:

"Hai Maliki."

"How did you know my name? "

"I have been expecting you."

"That's a little bit confusing."

"In what way?"

You couldn't possibly be expecting me if you have never seen me before and my guess is that you have not exactly heard about me either."

"That's the power of intuition for you."

"Not magic?"

"If you will call it that."

"For you to be expecting me means that someone would have told you about me and about what I was going to do."

"Like your secretary of state who you always call?"

"But that is not quite possible."

There was no way that Maliki would believe him. This

was the man who sent him out and beyond that he was the person coordinating the assignment on behalf of the entire world. Maybe this man was only trying to sow a seed of discord amongst his foes. On the other hand, nothing was impossible. This made him to remember a passage in his bible, which was to the effect that there was nothing new in anything that is done by man. Anything was possible. This was when the Israeli wise king Solomon was referred to as a preacher in the book of Ecclesiastes:

> *"The thing that hath been, it is that which shall be; and that which is done is that which shall be done: and there is no new thing under the sun*
>
> *"Is there any thing whereof it may be said, see, this is new? It hath been already of old time, which was before us."*
>
> (Ecclesiastes chapter 1 verses 9 and 10)

He had heard of double agents and he had heard of betrayals and so this might just be possible. It was Nidal that jolted him out of his thoughts with what he said next:

"Politics and reality are two different things mister Maliki, or should I say Ike?"

"I guess that I am one and the same person."

"You see Johnny splitter used to be my classmate, room mate and best friend in school."

"Who is Johnny splitter?"

"John Splitter is your secretary of state. That was his other name in school."

"I am still struggling with understanding how that could be possible."

"Then how else do you think that I know all about you?"

"That's what I am still trying to figure out."

"The sooner you succeed in figuring that out then the better it is for everyone involved."

"Just for curiosities' sake why did you go into those clandestine activities?"

"If you had read most of my messages, and I am sure that you have read them, then that question should not arise."

"Was it just about the inequality of nations and the political deception at the detriment of the masses?"

"That is the basic core of the matter. Your country for instance has its own way of life in which it insists that it is the best way. It also insists that God had fashioned their way of rulership, which is democracy, as the best for humans. I completely disagree with that notion. God had never been a democratic father. He makes the rules and it is for us to obey them. I am aware of the fact that you people insist that he also gave us the right or rather option to obey or disobey those rules. We should however not forget that there are punishments for those who disobey them. This in effect makes him a dictator and he always has our interest at heart. When for instance his people wanted to rule themselves, rather than him ruling them directly, he did not give them the option to choose a ruler. He simply gave them a king. It was not a parliament and there were no elections. To conduct elections was therefore a human invention in an attempt to go against God."

"I agree with you but that was god and we are humans."

"I also agree with you, but we are supposed to follow his examples. Apart from that, if you practice democracy then let it remain with you. Your aim had always been to force it on others especially those who prefer to follow the ways that god had set down. The idea of forcing it onto others immediately goes against the idea of democracy itself since force does not seem to be part of it. The use of force is an undemocratic process and yet that is what you people do. Apart from all this, you have killed too many people in this process both directly and indirectly. The rule by religious principles has been claimed by your people to always lead to wars and deaths but that does not seem to quite add up. Your attempts at the introduction of democracy have caused far more deaths than all the religious wars put together. Is it not therefore obvious that you are setting double standards?"

"You might be right there, but the use of force here is just as an agent of change."

"Be that as it may, the only thing that I have seen you people export successfully to the rest of the world is immorality. Most of the theocratic governments emphasize morality but you are for the opposite, and as humans, that seems to be what people want."

"If we are exporting immorality let that be because we have never tried to force anyone to accept them."

"You are not exactly right there. In the process of enforcing democracy the tendency is for you to tie up immorality with it, at least to make it more attractive. Besides that, this has been going on despite the fact that it is your religion that says that the path to the truth is narrow which means that it is hard, while that to hell is wide and easier. You have chosen to advertise the easier path. This is specifically stated by your bible, and to make it more imposing none other than your avatar himself said it:

> *"Enter ye in at the straight gate: for wide is the gate, and broad is the way, that leadeth to destruction, and many there be who go in thereat:*
>
> *"Because straight is the gate, and narrow is the way, which leadeth unto life, and few there be that find it."*
>
> (Matthew chapter 7, Verses 13 and 14.)

"It is therefore obvious that you are the custodians of that path to destruction which is the easier way of life, and as you tout it, people tend to go for it. Sex is the most touted and the most attractive of all these vices and you people have turned it into a pandemic of immorality."

"My guess is that I have to only reluctantly agree with you."

"If one could settle down and learn about others and try to understand their ways of life, cultures, their world views and ways of thinking, then it might become easier to change them. Any approach with these in mind will make their minds more malleable and so more easily susceptible towards the imbibitions of other foreign ways and the ability to change their own. It is this attitude of never trying to consider the ways of others that have made you and your ways detestable to many others."

Maliki knew better than to continue to listen to this man. He might not be able to convince him but he had a lot of valid ideas. He had come there to take him out and not to talk to him. It is always good never to underestimate ones opponent especially this type that seems to be very sly and wise. Then the man came clear. All this preaching was just to soften him up. He knew what he was planning. He suddenly changed the topic when he said:

"Incidentally I have an offer for you Mister Ike."

"What type of offer would that be?"

"You are a very brave, resourceful and fearless man. Why don't we just team up as partners? It will be a dynamite combination."

"Partnership in crime?"

"No. In money. For now I am worth over three trillion dollars, and with both of us together only the skies will be the limit."

"Are you trying to buy up my conscience?"

"No; just your expertise."

"My expertise is in fighting and I intend to try it out on your…"

He did not finish that sentence. Nidal had produced an Uzi Submachine gun out of nowhere and its muzzle was pointed at him. Maliki was well aware of the capabilities of that gun and so he simply dived to one side. He was lucky in that he had never underestimated this man's capabilities. He had been ready for any eventualities and was ready to react. In fact while talking he was only waiting for an opportunity to act himself, but Nidal seemed to be very careful too. The Uzi was spitting out hot lead while Agnes was already out and doing her own thing while still on the dive. This man was no easy target either. He was essentially on the move as he shot and moving targets were never easy to get at, particularly when they are as diminutive as this man. They continued to dodge and dive away from each other's path while firing, the Uzi having the upper hand, though it hindered his host's movement a little bit. Maliki had changed his clips on the dive and he kept squeezing one bullet after the other out of Agnes.

It eventually came down to a sort of drawn game. Each had exhausted his ammunition. Maliki had been hit on his left upper arm but it was just a graze, while Nidal got his own on his left thigh. The gun battle was over and it was time for hand-to-hand combat. Nidal was as much of a martial arts expert as Maliki, but Maliki had that edge over him. He was the master of any single move that one could conceive.

Though he had a very magnetic personality as well as an extraordinary intellect and an overbearing power of persuasion, other plans lay in wait for him. Fate and nemesis had permanently and intricately intertwined with each other to plot, dictate and effect his demise. The devil had perched on a nearby pedestal as his temporary altar with neither any liturgical nor burial vestments. He was there to make official and hasten his call to the nether world. It was going to be Nidal's final day on earth.

Nidal was the more nimble, probably because of his size, but Maliki was more of the ace than any other thing. Nidal came out flying towards him from across the room. Maliki swerved to one side and parried the kick with a left arm swipe. However Nidal's other leg caught him on his solar plexus. Intractable pain shot through his entire body but he was able to shut off the pain right away. He was also was able to maneuver his way out of the path of a karate chop that came for him. The chop instead, after missing him, landed on the table by his side and simply split it into two. Nidal was a fast fighter and Maliki took note of that. As Maliki therefore sidestepped, he let out a vicious instep to nowhere in particular. He got the little bastard on his knee and he heard the patella shatter. The man landed on the good leg as if nothing had happened and continued with the fight. It was obvious that he was there to fight to the end. He fought on as if he were just a robot.

By the time he came back on Maliki, it was to face a different foe. Maliki was already in a very foul mood. No man had ever given him such a fight and he was going to finish him up. He delivered a Polish bone crusher hammer blow as the man dived towards him. The combined velocity of his fists approaching the man and that of the man approaching him left the hammer blow with a great indeterminable force and effectiveness. It hit the man straight on his forehead and his fontanel split open. Maliki could see his brain heaving a breathe through the gap there as he fell to the floor almost lifeless. He did not want to take any chances and so he flew into the air and then let the leading edge of his right foot slash through his throat as he flew past. That virtually ripped off his Adams apple at the same time as his anno-rectal sphincter lost control. A vicious fart was released at the same time as his ungodly soul made its exit for hell.

He quickly planted his explosives there and left the place. The usual explosion and his signature took place from his car some ten minutes later on his way to the airport, and that was the end of the chapter on Nidal. The world had gotten rid of the devil in disguise that had terrorized all of civilization for well over two decades. He made a phone call to the secretary of state as soon as he was in the plane to inform him about the success of the operation. The secretary congratulated him and said that he was going to be at the airport in person to welcome him back.

Maliki, now Ike, did not want to create a scene whenever he got home and so he tried a little bit of psychological approach to the whole issue of the secretary of state. He informed him that he had intercepted virtually all his messages to Nidal. For that he intended to face him whenever he got home. The man did not reply to that before dropping the phone.

Ike returned home the following day. As he had expected the secretary of state had committed suicide and there was no suicide note. He let sleeping dogs lie and he never said a word as to what could have led to that suicide. Ike was welcomed back home as usual, and the United Nations Organization arranged and paid to him the staggering sum of five billion dollars for his single-handed effort which had more or less eliminated terrorism from the world. He attended the burial of the secretary of state and listened with much amusement to an eulogy. In this particular case, as he had expected, the eulogist did not disappoint him. He was not happy that the secretary of state was not alive to see his pet project come to fruition – the extermination of terrorism.

CPSIA information can be obtained at www.ICGtesting.com
Printed in the USA
BVOW04s0959151014

370934BV00001B/42/P

9 781432 771058